Let the Balloon Go

Let the Balloon Go

IVAN SOUTHALL

BRADBURY PRESS

New York

Bradbury Press
An Affiliate of Macmillan, Inc.
866 Third Avenue, New York, N.Y. 10022
Collier Macmillan Canada, Inc.
Manufactured in the United States of America
10 9 8 7 6 5 4 3 2 1
The text of this book is set in 12 pt. Century Old Style.

Library of Congress Cataloging in Publication Data:
Southall, Ivan.
    Let the balloon go.
    Summary: Handicapped by cerebral palsy and overprotected
by his parents, a twelve-year-old, left alone for the first time,
in a desperate need to exert his independence, does
precisely what he has been forbidden to do.
    [1. Cerebral palsy—Fiction. 2. Physically handicapped—Fiction] I. Title.
PZ7.S726Le 1984 [Fic] 85-5984
ISBN 0-02-786220-8

Let the Balloon Go is a work of fiction.
Any similarity to any person,
by name or nature, living or dead,
is coincidental.

Contents

1

John Clement Sumner

John Clement Sumner had a dreaming sort of feeling, a waking-up sort of feeling, an in-the-middle sort of feeling. It was like drifting in a boat in the eddies of a riverbank, lovely and lazy, and he didn't care whether his thoughts ran aground and went back to sleep or caught the current of the day. Though there was something out there in the day that was like a shadow, something or other, but he didn't know what, couldn't think of it, and didn't care. Then the sleepy thoughts all suddenly changed shape and went rushing away like startled cats down back alleys. He liked that; the *startled cats.* He'd stick them in an essay some time.

He lay there, sharp and wide awake, with his face half in the pillow, not sure whether to open his eyes or allow them to rove from side to side beneath closed lids.

Often he tried to see through his lids, but never could unless the light was bright. Then it was a red, luminous, hot, shapeless world that he saw (with mysterious animals in it like cells under a microscope), just as if he were in the midst of the sun, with no uphill or downhill, no left or right, no way in and no way out.

Once, in the garden, he had floundered round in that hot red world for five minutes or ten minutes (a very long time) fighting to escape from it, groping with his hands out in front of him until Mum had shrieked from the house, "John Sumner! What on earth are you doing? You'll be black and blue from bruises!"

But it wasn't a hot red world this morning; it was black; it was like being locked up in a box full of curious noises that didn't make sense. He concentrated on those noises but couldn't hear them properly because one ear was buried way down deep in the pillow, and really and truly he didn't want to *look*. *Looking* often spoilt the game, particularly before he was sure what the game was going to be. A fellow had to give himself time to get the plan straight. Sometimes a game came. Sometimes he gave up.

As quietly as he could manage it he twisted over onto his back in the creaking bed (the blooming thing, as always, groaning like a door) and pressed the palms of his hands flat and hard into the mattress. Going taut like that was part of the drill for hearing things; it was also a super position for leaping out of bed, and when John Clement Sumner leapt he leapt like a gazelle.

"You're terrific," the kids used to say, "the things you can do."

Even things like leaping into the air from off his back; a mighty contortion, then straight up! But it wasn't time for gymnastics yet, though very soon it would be time for something. He could *feel* it, that buildup of tension, that tightening, that certainty inside him that a terrific idea was only a moment or two away.

Little by little he began to isolate the sounds he could hear by forcing his eyelids still harder together (the way it was when you listened to music very intently); parrots and mynas and magpies, and an incredible mixture of chirpings and cheepings from all sorts of insects and birds, an awful row they made all of them together, notably the parrots, squawking and clicking their beaks like busy old women knitting. Somewhere a boy with an axe was splitting wood for his mother's kitchen stove: creepy Sissy Parslow probably—the chopping sound was too feeble for a manly boy. Not that anyone but the Parslows had an old-fashioned stove; it was practically prehistoric. The Parslows spent their money on motorcars and didn't have enough left for stoves. Somewhere else a noisy dog, or two dogs, or three: those blooming little terriers at Percy Mullen's place—fools of dogs like toys; and scratching sounds that might have been human or animal or, less likely, wind.

If, in a casual sort of way, you took no notice, the morning seemed to be peaceful, but if a fellow listened like mad there were noises everywhere. Awfully strange noises, really; awfully peculiar noises; and he was a little afraid that his imagination would gallop away like a horse. Already he could hear an echo of Mum's regular wail, "John Clement Sumner, your imagination will be the death of me."

John shivered a little and sat up and almost against his will opened his eyes. There was a feeling in him that it had stopped being a game, that this was not a game day, that this was a real day, that there was a shadow in it.

It was daylight outside, sunlight, and something about the curtains was awfully odd. They were heaving as if someone had taken up a standing position against the wall behind them. ("Careful, John Sumner. Of course no one's there.") It was a movement as though from kneecaps and elbows, as if the person there had wearied of standing and had tried to ease an ache.

Then his narrowing gaze darted nervily to the wardrobe. The door there was open, but should have been shut. It was always shut at night. He *never* slept with the wardrobe door open.

Was he imagining it or was it real? He wasn't sure any more.

Surely he hadn't left the wardrobe ajar!

Was there a thief in the room? Was someone *really* behind those curtains? Crikey. Had he disturbed the thief when he had turned onto his back and braced his hands, flat and hard, into the mattress? Was the movement in the curtain not from a person getting tired, but from someone who had rushed into hiding?

A shiver went up and down his spine and he was muddled for an awful period of blankness when he could not really remember how it had all started, whether he had started it himself as a game or not. It was desperate the way a fellow's mind could empty out like a drain. Fragments of thought rushed this way and that trying to picture something valuable enough to bring a thief into the room where he slept. Not his model yacht; not his project about cheeses; not his encyclopedia of ten volumes. He could see them all and they hadn't been touched.

Then his thoughts leapt to Mr. Robert Macleod, that shadow in the background waiting to spoil the day. Yes; Macleod it was, that horrible man, who for some ridiculous reason always wore a hat even indoors—unless he had to wear a hat to hide his horns! A devil was Mr. Robert Macleod, and was this more of his devilry? That bullying man, that wheedling man, that torturer who got other men with knives to do his dirty work, that horrible creep who talked in a bloodless and confident way of *invisible* things when the whole idea was stupid.

He didn't want to think any more about Macleod and he tried harder and harder to drag his eyes away from the curtains, but they fascinated him and something about them was very strange and very perturbing. Someone was there, behind them, of that he was sure, but there weren't any feet at the bottom. No feet. *No feet!*

The rays of the sun were strong and there should have been a shadow on the curtain but there was not. The intruder could not possibly have got out. The fly-wire screen was in place to stop him, and the screen could not be moved from inside the room, only from outside the house.

There were no feet *because* there was no shadow; it was as simple as that. But invisibility for people, even for Macleod and his henchmen, was absolute rot. "Invisible," Macleod had said, *"invisible,* lad."

But now he could only stare and break into a sweat and wrench his eyes away and dart them from point to point looking for something to hit the intruder with. A fishing rod was there, a door stop, and that knobbled old walking-stick left to him when Grandma died. ("What do I want a walking-stick for?" he had wailed at the time.)

But looking for a weapon started off a tremble inside him that he was unable to stop; yet wasn't John Clement Sumner the toughest kid about town? He could outrun anybody, outfight the lot, swing from a rope like a monkey (it made them gasp), even ride his bike up that whopping great hill near Gifford's place, and there wasn't another kid in miles who could get halfway to the top.

"You're terrific," the kids used to say, "the things you can do."

He would have to use that walking-stick, whether Grandma's ghost shrieked or not, swung with all his might, head high, *crack*. But did he dare to move at all? Who was to say the intruder would not strike back?

Should he call for help? Should he bring other people into it? Should he call out something like, "Dad. Quick. He's here. He didn't wait for me to go to him. He's here. Knife and all. They're going to do me in."

But it was too late for that, and he was dismayed by the bedroom clock. The hands were at 7:25. Dad had left for town. There wasn't a man in the house. But Dad wouldn't have known what it was all about. By the time he had pulled himself together (he was so slow in the mornings, so painfully, ridiculously slow) the intruder would have broken out through the fly-wire screen and vanished into the garden. An invisible man on the loose would never be found out there, or would he leave footprints on the grass? Would plants and bushes move as he rushed past?

Would he leave signs as he dodged this way and that? No mere man, invisible or not, was fast enough to dodge John Clement Sumner in a chase. Or might John bring him down with a hard-flung stone? *Crack.* Like David cracked Goliath flat on his back.

Then when this character lay stretched on the grass, felled by that stone, would the potion that made him invisible begin to wear off? Completely visible then, or half-visible like a ghost? Would it be Macleod himself, or one of his henchmen, or some subhuman monster made by evil-thinking men, by reckless experimenters who (in Dad's words) "release madness on the earth and accept no blame for anything they do"?

Then Mum came into the room. "Hullo, dear," she said, "you're a sleepyhead this morning."

She stepped to the windows and threw the curtains wide. *Crash.* They clattered on the rods. It was a wonder they didn't take off and go into orbit. It was like being hit on the head with a sheet of breaking glass.

"It's a lovely morning out there," she said, as sweet as pie. "Let's invite it in."

John smiled thinly (so thinly that he looked like someone about to be sick), but flared up inside. He felt like murder, like smashing something, like screaming, but moaned in the pit of his stomach, way down deep, where no one could hear his words. "Oh, Mum, did you have to do that? What's wrong with you? Didn't you know? Couldn't you guess? Couldn't you see that it was a real beaut game?"

His adventure fell down like a building hit by bombs (as seen on TV): a shower of bricks, splitting walls toppling, clouds of choking dust, wailing sirens and explosions. Before he'd even got it right; she'd wrecked it before he had sorted it all out and made it into a world-beater.

He slumped in a disappointment of emptiness.

2

Grown-ups Don't Have to Hear

Mum had this terribly childish habit—when John was around—of addressing the time of day as if it were a person. "Good morning, Morning." "Good middle to you, Noon." "Good evening to you, Night." It was enough to drive a fellow up the wall.

He was twelve two weeks ago; it was kids' stuff, talking to the time of day. There was nothing more pathetic than a grown-up being stupid. Did she think it was going to answer back or something? ("Hi-ya, Mrs. Sumner.") Just for once he wished it would; she'd faint dead away from fright.

Sure enough, there she stood as usual beaming

sweetly at the sunshine. "Good morning, Morning. Kindly step inside. It's time you dragged this lazy imp out by the scruff of his neck."

"For crying out loud, Mum. Turn it off."

"Run along to your shower, John."

He rolled his eyes at the ceiling. "Aw. . .Heck!"

"Breakfast in ten minutes. We're in a hurry this morning, remember?"

"Why?"

"You know why."

"Blooming town," he groaned. "I hate town. Have I got to go? Can't I stay home? Town's for women, not for kids."

"No," she said, "you can't stay home." Then pecked him on the cheek and was suddenly gone, *laughing*, leaving the window behind her, open and empty and bright with sunlight.

John scowled at it, at the shreds of the invisible ghost of the nothing he had built his adventure on. Nothing was left except the garden outside, parrots feasting like pirates in the apple tree, mynas bathing with a flurry of wings in a clamshell, brier roses blazing as though on fire, feathery silver birch trees rippling like seawater to a change of wind.

"A hundred times *blow* it. It was working up to be a real beauty. Then in she comes!"

He groaned. A whole day with nothing to do but tag around like a dog on a lead, with nothing to do but stand and wait, with nothing to do but sit, with no one to see except Mr. Blooming Macleod.

"I hate town."

He spilled himself from the bed and shuffled to the bathroom, trailing his dressing-gown by a single sad sleeve.

"Like Dad says," he grumbled, harping back to his adventure, "the finer things are for men. Women don't understand. Shakespeare was a man. Michelangelo was a man. Mozart was a man. The Beatles were men. Women are slobs."

He poked out his tongue and regarded it in the bathroom mirror—a habit he had acquired from Dad. "Urrgh," he said, just like Dad (though John's tongue was as pink as a bright new day), then peeled off his pyjamas and turned on the shower.

"Put your head under," Mum shouted from the kitchen. "Get some water in your ears."

"For Pete's sake," he moaned, "will they ever leave you alone? I'm not a little kid any more. And still she tells me all the time. Just because the rest of the family's grown up and gone away she thinks I've got to stay a baby till I'm an old man."

He leant back and looked critically at himself in the

mirror again: tanned and glowing from the heat of a long summer, square-jawed, black-haired, brown-eyed. He liked the look of himself in that particular mirror—he always had. He looked more like a man than a boy in that mirror because it showed only his head. Some kids looked more like babies or little girls, pretty-pretty, but not John Clement Sumner, no, sir-ree.

Kids used to say sometimes, "You're terrific; the things you can do." (That made him feel good, made him glow; the kids knew it, too.)

He had overheard grown-ups say, "The strength of character and courage in that boy's face. He's going to make his mark, no mistake."

Others had said, "He's a clever kid. Of course he ought to be; you know what his father is, and his mother's a bright one. She still helps out at the university with a lecture or two."

But there was the day when Sissy Parslow had sneered, "How can he be clever? I bet his mother does his homework for him. Doesn't she, Johnny boy?"

"She doesn't. She bally well doesn't. I'll punch you in the nose, Sissy Parslow."

"Or maybe his daddy does it for him. 'What's two

and two, Daddy, so everyone can think I'm clever at school?'"

"I don't call him Daddy. You're a real creep, Sissy Parslow. I hate the sight of you, Sissy Parslow."

It was a terrific fight. It was murder, the kids said. Sissy Parslow had to go to the doctor to be stuck together again. John, to his surprise, was sorry about it. It was almost like watching himself being beaten to a pulp. In the end he had to run away from it, so the kids had dropped Sissy over a fence and left him there to wail, but Sissy only had himself to blame. He shouldn't have picked on John Clement Sumner in the first place; that was what the kids said.

"John! Are you under that shower?"

He groaned. "Yes, Mum."

"You're not just standing beside it, pretending?"

"Of course not."

"Well, how is it that you can hear me?"

(Wouldn't it make you sick?)

He mumbled a few words he wasn't brave enough to say louder and held out an arm to get wet.

"John!" Her voice was suddenly against his ear and he nearly dropped from fright.

"Gee," he yelled, "fair go, Mum! That's a shockin' thing to do."

"I'll fair-go you, young fellow." She planted his right hand firmly on the shower rail, took him by an ear, and propelled him under the water.

"It's cold!" he shrieked.

"Cold, fiddlesticks," she said; "it's practically boiling. Use the soap. Go on. Slosh it round your neck and ears. I'm not taking you to town smelling like a polecat."

"Please, Mum," he shrieked. "It's too hot!"

"Hot, fiddlesticks," she said; "it's practically freezing."

"You'd say anything, wouldn't you? First it's hot, then it's cold. I'll dob you in, that's what I'll do. I'll tell the Girl Guides their bloomin' commissioner's a big fibber."

She turned the taps off.

"Dry yourself," she said, "properly! There's a clean shirt in your wardrobe. Wear your suit."

"Aw, Mum, that bloomin' old suit. It's a sunny day. I hate suits. Suits are for men, not for kids."

"And we'll have underpants and a singlet, thank you. And clean socks, you dirty little demon. There's plenty of everything in your drawer."

"Can't I stay home, Mum, just this once?"

"I do wish you'd not ask that ridiculous question."

Her eyes got that glazed look all of a sudden. "Nothing would give me greater pleasure than a day in the city without you; it'd be sheer heaven; but it's not to be my good fortune, as you well know."

"Please, Mum!" he yelled after her. "I hate town. I hate standing around. It's cruel making me stand around. People always stare when a fellow stands around. It's not nice being stared at. Can we go by train? Have we got to take the car?"

But she was back in the kitchen and suddenly stone deaf.

"Mum," he yelled.

She ignored him. Grown-ups didn't have to hear when they didn't want to. They were different from kids.

"Mum," he yelled, "I've dropped me dressing-gown in the wet."

No reply.

"Can I have cold milk on my Wheaties instead of hot?"

No reply.

Never, never would she give him cold milk like other kids got every day of their lives. Hot milk made it all mushy, like pig swill.

"Can I have a fried egg instead of a boiled one?"

No reply.

Boiled eggs were the absolute end. Boiled eggs and bread and butter. Other kids had bacon with eggs fried in fat; they had sausages and pancakes, all good and greasy, sloshed over with tomato sauce.

"Can I have a dollar to spend when we get to town?"

Silence. By golly, grown-ups were rough. If a kid didn't answer when he was spoken to he was slapped down.

He shuffled back to his room.

"Mum! Where'd you say my shirt was?"

A few moments later, "I haven't got any clean socks."

A little later still, "I've got a tear in the pants of me suit."

That brought her running. She came roaring down the passage like a runaway truck. "You've got *what?*"

"See," he said.

She screeched, "How did you do that?"

"I dunno."

"John! It's inches long."

"Yeh."

"I could never mend a great tear like that. It's a tailor's job; I'd ruin them if I tried. How long has it been there, you naughty boy?"

(Ooh; that *naughty boy* made him see red.)

"I dunno. I felt a bit of a draft on Sunday."

"You *never* wore them to church like that?"

"Suppose I did. Must have done. How can I remember?"

"But surely you noticed?"

"I can't see round there, can I? I haven't got eyes in me bottom."

"Enough of *that*, young man, thank you very much. *That* is a vulgarity and you'll not be common in this house."

It was going to be a real beaut day. It had all the signs; even that set look on Mum's face. It was set like an easterly wind, bleak and stormy. Then she sighed. "Boys, boys, boys. Sad is the lot of woman with nothing but sons. Why couldn't I have had a nice quiet little girl to finish up with?"

It was a confusing sort of statement, but Mum was like that. A fellow never knew where he was with her. When she seemed to be all steamed up to tear him limb from limb she'd suddenly go all weepy or dewy or luvvie-duvvie.

"I suppose you'll have to wear your school trousers," she said.

"They're dirty."

"The other pair, boy. You *know* the pair I mean."

"Can't. They're in the wash."

Her mood changed again; it was like a seesaw: wham, wham; from one face to the other.

"You are downright irritating this morning, John. What on earth has got into you? You're so *rude* and I'm just not up to it."

He grimaced at that and knew he was being rude in a way, but somehow couldn't stop it.

"I've got far too much on my mind, John. I've got lectures to worry about; I've got you to worry about. They are *not* in the wash."

"But they are. You didn't wash them because I don't go back to school till Friday, because it's Teachers' Conference today and tomorrow. They're soaking in the machine where you told me to put them."

She ran a hand through her hair and an oddly frantic look came to her eyes. "Put on what you've got then. Why should I care? I don't care what you wear as long as you're decent. Then get up to the table before your breakfast ruins."

He slumped on the bed and felt properly mad; about what, apart from Mum, he wasn't sure. It was one of those days all right; one of those real beaut days that always ended up in a rip-roaring row, with everyone in it, Dad, too, with Mum crying in her room, with Dad trying to hush her in case someone came to the door and heard, with all sorts of things said that would hurt afterwards for days; with everyone being sorry about it, and wishing the words had never been said.

When he arrived in the kitchen hoping for miracles she took a hard look at him.

"That's that, isn't it? I hope you're proud of yourself. How can you be seen like that? How can we go to town? I couldn't drag you along looking like that. What on earth do you do with your clothes? Clean the car with them? Wipe the floor with them? How can you possibly be covered in mud when it hasn't rained for a month?"

"Hot milk," he grumbled. "I asked for cold."

"You need hot milk. Hot milk is the rule. What am I to do with you, John? You're really beyond me at times."

He wasn't supposed to answer that and couldn't have done if he had tried.

"I *must* go to town today. I have my lecture. I have the papers to go back to Mr. Macleod and I intend to deliver them in person." She was pretty far gone; she was in a right, royal fizz. "You'll have to sit in the car at the parking station and like it and lump it."

"Fair go," he wailed.

"You should have thought of that when you ripped your trousers."

"I'll bet it'll be in that basement again, stuck there for hours and hours like last time. With nothin' to look at and nothin' to do. You'll bloomin' well leave me *there* on my own, won't you, but you won't leave me here on my own."

She sighed, not once, but two or three times; even ran her hand through her hair again, disarranging it. Last time she had left him in the basement parking station it had been only for an hour or so in the morning; this time it would be for most of the day. She began to argue with herself. "How am I to break these appointments? I'm lecturing at ten-thirty and lecturing is not a whim. I must be there. I'm seeing Mr. Macleod at two and he's expecting me. With him there are things to discuss; important things, John, as you know. Matters of such importance cannot be discussed over the telephone; one cannot write letters about them. They must be discussed face to face."

John could have moaned aloud from the misery that was mixed up with the name of Mr. Robert Macleod.

"Nor will Mrs. Walton be here to look after you. I told her I wouldn't need her and she said that suited her particularly well. It would be a change for her to have a Wednesday at home. She's so very good, John; I can't go back on my word. If ever I lose Mrs. Walton I don't know what we'll do. I'd have to give up everything and that wouldn't be good for me or for you. It's a strain for a mother, John; she's got to have a change of scene."

He looked at her appealingly, with large dark eyes, and didn't realize how deep that appeal was, how starkly she saw it, how much it wrenched at her. "Let me stay, Mum, just this once. I won't make a mess or break anything. Honest I won't. Not all day trailing round or sitting in that rotten car, Mum. Would you like it: sitting all day in a car in a basement?"

"I can't leave you here." Her voice was tired, almost frail.

"What's the difference? If you'll leave me there, why can't you leave me here?"

"Oh, John; how many more times? There's all the difference in the world. I'm close to you there, never more than a few blocks away. But from here it's thirty miles to town. If anything happened I'd never forgive myself."

"What *can* happen?" Her mouth opened but he rushed on. "Gee, I'm not a baby any more. I'm not really sick or anything. The worst I can get is the shakes. Why should it happen here any more than in the car?"

She sat opposite him, drumming the table with a finger. "Now listen to me. Why can't you understand? This is what Mr. Macleod says—*why can't you understand?* If you're in the car you're resting; you're not running wild; my mind's at peace. I know while you're resting I needn't worry. Here, heaven alone knows what you'd be up to. You'd be getting yourself excited; rushing about. Of course you're not sick, not really, but only because . . . only because . . ."

She was distressed. There were things she couldn't say to him. Although he was twelve, he was "spastic," and easily hurt by careless words.

"John, I'll be away for more than five minutes, much more than for an hour or two. I can't be back before half-past four, not even allowing for traffic that may delay me, and it's your father's late night. He won't be home until heaven knows when."

"I'll be all right here, Mum, really I will. It'll be beaut."

"I think perhaps I'd better drop you off at Auntie

Vi's. I should have thought of it before. It solves all our problems."

"Oh golly, not that. There's no one to play with there. It's deadly at Auntie Vi's."

"There's no one to play with here, either, is there?"

"One of the kids might come. There's no school while the teachers are away." But he knew the kids wouldn't come. Kids wanted fun. There wasn't much fun at the Sumners'. "I don't care, anyway. I've got lots to do. I can get on with my project. I can do my model."

She was silent, but restless. He could see it in the way her fingers were working and she was beginning to look worried. She often looked worried, but not quite like this; never exactly in this way before.

"Dad says you've got to start leaving me. He's always saying it. He says you can't make a slave of yourself for ever."

Still she didn't say anything and now all the fingers of her right hand were drumming the table-top and he knew, *suddenly,* that she was thinking of giving in.

"Mum, Mum. Please."

He had broken through that terrible wall of indifference, that blank barrier that grown-ups lived behind with their eyes shut and their ears closed to almost everything that a fellow said.

"Please, Mum. Please, Mum."

He felt a terrific surge of excitement, of wonder, of release.

"I'll be all right. You'll see. Please, Mum, please, please."

She came round to him, put a hand on his shoulder, then suddenly kissed his hair. "Very well." And walked with a peculiar gait from the room, as though hundreds of eyes were watching her. "I'll get myself ready," she said.

He couldn't believe it.

Suddenly, he couldn't grasp it any more and felt stunned.

"She'll change her mind; I know she will; but she mustn't, she mustn't change her mind. Oh please, Jesus; please, please, please."

3

A Flock of Starlings

At the gateway a copse of cherry-plum trees met in an arch, and Mrs. Sumner's busy little car bustled out through it. In a moment she would be back; John was sure of it. Back she'd come and everything hoped for would melt away. She called as she went, "I'll ring you from Melbourne to see how you are, so don't go away from home."

Her eyes still had that slightly frantic look. "Don't be ridiculous," she had snapped on another occasion, "one cannot be *slightly* frantic, and I'm not frantic anyway, not even slightly."

But she was.

It was a rather wild sort of look that made her hands restless and quickened her movements and shortened her breath. John always knew when she was like it, even if he couldn't see her, because he could hear it in her voice.

It happened often round five or six o'clock in the evening when her sense of fun seemed suddenly to run out without warning, or oddly on Sunday mornings when she was getting him ready for Sunday School, or when certain visitors were expected to call.

Sometimes Dad would say to her, "Easy, old dear." Other times Dad would lose patience and there would be a rip-roaring row. Then Mum would rush to another room and sob and John would hear his name mentioned and Dad would try to keep her quiet. "Be quiet, be quiet," he'd say; "if anyone comes to the door we'll never live it down."

There hadn't been a row or sobbing this time because Dad wasn't at home to start it off, but Mum's voice had become more and more breathless.

Before she had stepped into the car she had said, "If you turn on taps make sure you turn them off. Don't use the steam iron or the vacuum cleaner or the washing machine, and leave your father's tools in the shed. I don't want you electrocuting yourself or cutting an arm off. For heaven's sake don't climb anything."

Earlier than that she had said, "When the baker comes get a packet of buns. They'll be nice for your lunch. There's plenty of milk in the fridge, so don't go fooling with the kitchen stove."

She had tried to provoke an argument, tempting him to rebel against her (John could sense it), so that she could order him to go with her as a punishment. "Wash your hands before lunch. Brush your teeth after lunch. Keep out of the fowl-house; your father hasn't had time to clean it. Don't use the garden hose or weed the flower beds; your father will kill you if you weed the flower beds, because you always pull up the flowers. Don't pick the good roses; your father counts the blooms. I know I shouldn't be leaving you; I'm sure it's a dreadful mistake; I feel it in my bones."

She had also managed to say as she had darted round the house gathering up the things she had to take to town, "I've drawn the curtains in case the day gets hot. Have a nap in the afternoon whether you feel tired or not. Don't go inviting that dreadful Mullen boy into the house if he happens along. Don't let the budgie out of his cage or you'll never catch him. Don't eat green apples off the tree."

Even as she had gone out to the car she had added, "I shouldn't be leaving you. It's not right whether your father says it is or it isn't. I'm the one who has to live with the worry all the time. Your father's off to work every day and your brothers scarcely ever set foot in the place. It's different for them; they can put it out of their heads. The responsibility's *mine*. For my sake you'll just have to come with me and sit in the car."

"No, Mum. *Please, Mum.*"

He knew she had a battle to fight, but not in the way that he had to. He knew that being the mother of a boy like himself was not like being the mother of an ordinary boy. Ordinary boys had arms and legs that did the right things; John's arms and legs only sometimes did the right things; and when Mum got upset about it John usually got worse. He would start ·stumbling and dropping things and stammering, and sometimes had to beat his thigh with his fist over and over again, very hard, to get out his words. His heart would pound like a hammer and sometimes (to his own horror) he would cry. Other times the same thing would happen for no reason at all. Once it had happened in church, but at school it had happened many times. Sometimes he got over it; or the headmaster would ring Mum and she would rush down in the car to take him home.

But this morning it hadn't happened. She had got upset, but he had come through all right. He had prayed for the tremble not to start, for his words to come easily, for his arms and legs to do exactly as he wished, and everything had been fine. Then with her hand to the door of the car she had said, "If you feel that anything might go wrong ring the parsonage or Police Constable Baird. Don't wait for it to happen. Get on that telephone as soon as you feel it coming. If one number doesn't answer try the other. . . ."

"You know nothing'll go wrong, Mum."

"Promise, promise."

"I promise."

She had stared, not really seeing him, then pulled herself together, smiled, kissed him, squeezed his shoulder as she often did, and after a jerky start, backed the car out of the drive. Usually, she drove very well. Then from under the arch of cherry-plum trees she had called, "I'll ring from Melbourne to see how you are, so don't go away from home."

John listened to the engine note fade; it was like a storm blowing away; like a violent night turning into a morning of calm. But would the storm swing about and blow back?

He didn't know that his face was strained, that his

fists were clenched, that his eyes were half-shut. He knew of nothing except the nerve tremble in his knees and the flutter in his innards.

"Please, please send her away. Don't let her come back."

She didn't come back.

Gradually he heard birds again and barking dogs and bees and children shouting somewhere. They had never sounded the same before. There was the sound of freedom and wide open spaces in them. They were like a proud anthem that he had never learnt to sing. He had always been a listener, always separate, always apart; had never been able to sing the same music with the same spirit for himself. Now perhaps he could.

That arch of cherry-plum trees remained empty, quite empty, like a fishbowl upended, upside down, emptied out. Like a fishbowl from which the fish (grown too big) had been taken down to the creek and let go. Oh, imagine that fish set free, bewildered by rivers of water, miles upstream, miles down; free to go wherever it wished. Or would it be like the budgie released for the first time from its cage, sitting on top of the cage in the living room, huddled against it, cowering, trying to get back inside? The budgie was only a bird; the fish was only a fish; John Clement Sumner was a *boy*.

Mum had gone. She had not come back.

His body seemed to fill with fragrant, cooling oils and he looked up through the trees to the sky. He loved the sky. A flock of starlings scared up from somewhere drummed overhead. Each bird, each one, flew away as with a link broken from the chains that had held him from the day he had been born. He could almost see the chains break up, could almost feel them go.

In that beautiful moment he flushed to a tremendous excitement, yet there was a sense of calm and contentment unlike anything he had known. All the tremble washed out beneath it. Inside he was like a sea at evening, no gales there, no waves, no breakers of discontent.

"Fly away, birds!" he cried, and each link borne by a bird was something his mother or his father or his grown-up brothers or a doctor or a nurse or a schoolteacher or a policeman had told him that he, especially, was not to do.

"You must remember that you are different from other children. You can never be sure that your limbs will obey you. It's no one's fault that you're 'spastic';

no one can be blamed; least of all yourself; but we've all got to learn to live with it. If we ignore some things they go away, but if we ignore this or if you ignore it we may have serious accidents on our hands. Other children, particularly, sometimes expect too much of you. They may put you into dangerous situations even though they don't mean to. Perhaps even dangerous for them and doubly dangerous for you.

"You mustn't chop wood or use a saw or hammer nails or swing on the monkey bars or ride a bike or get into fights or play football or cricket or softball or rough games with boys or girls in case you injure yourself. You mustn't run fast in case you fall. You mustn't go near the edge of cliffs or climb trees or ladders in case you overbalance. You mustn't play with matches or boiling water or this or that or the next thing.

"Of course there are lots of things you can do and we must be thankful for that, mustn't we? You don't, after all, have to go to a special school. You can swim in shallow water if someone is with you. You can go fishing with your friends as long as one of them will bait your hook. You can go for nice walks with other people. You can be timekeeper for the football team and scorer for the cricket team and they're both very important jobs. You can see all the beauty of the world around you. You can read books and watch TV and listen to music and collect things. And you do have a marvellous imagination. With that there is almost nothing you cannot do. In your imagination you can swim the broadest river, run the fastest race, climb the highest mountain—and believe you me, lad, the adventures of the mind in the long run are far more exciting than the adventures of the body."

How stupid it was, all those grown-up words, all those grown-up meanings. How could they expect him to *like* it? Even when they were telling him about the things he could do they were saying it in such a way that the fun was about as joyful as a stab of toothache. And when he did use his imagination, as they said he should, someone would end up shouting, "John Clement Sumner, your imagination will be the death of me."

It made him sick and they thought he didn't mind; patted him on the head and called him a good boy (perhaps he should purr), squeezed his shoulders and smiled at him, told him he was wonderful, he was clever, he was brave. But all the time they were only telling him that he was different, was as good as useless, was a dreadful worry to everybody, was half a boy, not a whole boy, was a peculiar little object known as John Clement Sumner who had to be handled carefully like a broken egg.

Sometimes he thought he would explode. Bang. And someone would have to rush round with a broom to sweep up a billion bits.

Surely by now they should have guessed that he was a whole boy bound hand and foot, that they had made his body into a prison, that he was a young lion in chains, that he was an eagle with clipped wings, that he was really a Charles Lindbergh, an Edmund Hillary, a *Hercules*? Didn't they know that a balloon was not a balloon until someone cut the string?

Even Mr. Robert Macleod didn't know that much and he was supposed to know everything. All he could do was put on a patient face: "You're handicapped, lad, and you're of an age when you should begin to understand what cerebral palsy means in relation to yourself. You're an odd sort of case. Name any aspect of it, spastic, athetoid or ataic, and you seem to have it, but none to excess. In some ways you're very fortunate. I know of many boys and girls much simpler to diagnose, but far worse off.

"There are some terrible things, lad. They'd break your heart. I sometimes think that everyone should see these people who suffer great afflictions. The human spirit tormented beyond belief is a wonderful thing.

"As for you, you're intelligent, you have an artistic temperament, you have gifted and loving parents who encourage your talents and who surround you with the civilized things that help to make a real man. Physically, the exercises you've been doing seem not to have been a waste of time, but I would like you to try harder, even when it hurts. It is by getting to know our weaknesses, rather than our strengths, that the big leap forward is made."

(The way he talked! He was the same as the rest of them. And what did they really know about it? They weren't boys themselves. They weren't *handicapped* themselves.)

"Your parents and I have been talking about surgeons again. I'm sure they will be able to make your left leg less bothersome for you and that will assist the right leg. They can rearrange a few things. Really, lad, your fear of this operation is without logic. Nothing will be visible from the outside. No one will ever know that it has been done—unless you tell them—

and when you become more confident on your feet many of the other things that trouble you may be a lot easier to live with. It's my job to know about these things and I *do* know. I *do* know what goes on inside the mind of a handicapped boy, just as other men, the surgeons, know what goes on inside your body. We're going to take some X-rays, then the surgeons, clever men, very clever men indeed, will decide with me whether the operation can be done now or perhaps later when you have grown a little more. Your parents are anxious to sign the papers, but they haven't forced their wishes on you before and they're not forcing you now. What do you say?"

"Is it going to hurt?"

He had looked surprised. "Hurt? There could be slight discomfort for a while; it would not be fair of me to say otherwise; but that's not the point, lad. Nothing worth getting ever comes without effort."

"What will they do inside my leg?"

"I have told you. A snip here and a snip there and things of that nature. Nothing you have to worry about. You'll never see it nor will anyone else. Your mother and father will fill you in on the details when you're old enough to understand."

"I'm old enough to understand now."

"I say you're not."

"But if it's not a success I won't be able to walk any better, will I? And I'll have an invisible mix-up inside my leg and a great big scar on the outside."

"No; I have told you no. We wouldn't do that sort of thing to you. We wouldn't operate if we thought we couldn't succeed. I know hundreds of boys who'd love to wear a neat and tidy scar, like a medal, like a badge of honour."

"Not me."

All the way home Mum and Dad were silent and miserable and twice he caught Mum glancing at him guiltily. "You're not going to sign those papers, are you, Mum?"

But they did. It was done.

John was sure that Mr. Robert Macleod must have been the spitting image of creepy Sissy Parslow as a kid.

He stood on the open driveway looking up at branches and leaves and sky, with his chains gone (wonderful, wonderful), with his blood running wild, and with that busy little car of Mum's completely gone, bustling far away through the hills down to Melbourne.

"Oh, golly," he almost yelled. "It can't be true."

For this one day he had waited all his life. Every day lived had been counted simply as one more along the road to this one. Oh, it was fierce; it was crazy.

He would run like the wind, he would leap and dance, he would cartwheel and swing from trees. All these things he would do because there was no one to tell him that he could not do them, because there were no hidden eyes peering at him through the curtain, no shrill voice: "John, get down from there!" "John, walk, don't run!" Mum's voice, Dad's voice, Mrs. Walton's voice, every blooming voice a fellow ever heard.

They were wrong, all of them but one.

He could do anything that any boy could do: kick a football, hit a cricket ball out of sight, swim a hundred yards, dive into deep water, dig a dirty great hole, fight fist and tooth and claw, sit on the topmost branch and shriek at the sky.

It was only the look in their eyes and the things they said that stopped him. He couldn't do them because he never tried, because they frightened him with looks and words, because they said, "You mustn't. No, John. Don't."

Slicing him open and rearranging things inside wouldn't make any difference. What a horrible idea;

what a terrible thing to do. Maybe they'd put something in there: an IT. *Something* that wasn't part of himself. It'd be worse than false teeth: those awful leering contraptions that Dad took out at night and popped in a glass of water. You could hear them hit the side of the glass from all over the house. Things like that weren't going to make any difference. Someone had said that once, in a roundabout way; some unknown, gentle-eyed man who had spoken to him on a city street.

John had been standing there trembling, trying to fight off the shakes, waiting for Mum who never seemed to be coming. The man's head had come down, his eyes had come down, and then his voice like a quiet fire: "You'll do it, son. Don't let anything stop you from being the boy you want to be. The answer's inside you. A balloon is not a balloon until you cut the string and let it go."

4

Let the Balloon Go

Well, he wouldn't be doing his stupid old project or his stupid old model, not even because he had said he would, not even to make Mum happy. They could rot; they could burst into flames. A plastic model of 227 pre-cut pieces stuck together with knobs and slots and dobs of glue, because he wasn't allowed to make a real model out of wood with knives and chisels; a project about stupid old cheese on a smudged piece of card (30 inches by 24 inches) with words and pictures cut from magazines.

"You know you can't print your own words properly because you can't hold a pen for any length of time without your hand shaking and going all silly, and you don't want to spoil your project, do you?"

Could he slip off into Sherbrooke Forest and find lyre-birds and wombats and wallabies and anteaters and possums?

Could he take his rod and fish in the Sassafras Creek on the way?

Could he dig a hole in the yard, a big deep hole like the other boys dug?

Like the big hole in Percy Mullen's backyard that was a smuggler's cave, a gold mine, a fortress, a volcanic crater, the Colosseum with the lions roaring for their tea. It had places in it for secret things. It was a club room. It was a real, beaut hole. In winter it filled with water and was then the Pacific Ocean, or the Bay of Bengal, or a sinking ship with all hands to the pumps. It was dangerous, too, and Mr. Mullen was always going to fill it in, but didn't. Maybe Mr. Mullen remembered that he had been a boy.

Could he climb onto the roof and sit on the ridge? The roof was always there like a mountain, like the Matterhorn, like an Everest, conquered by others but not himself. Percy Mullen not only sat on roofs but jumped off them as well, but Percy was allowed to do almost anything, even chop down trees.

Sissy Parslow had sat on his roof. "I'm the king of the castle," Sissy had jeered, "and you're the dirty rascal."

Sissy was a creep.

John saw the flock of starlings come back (those starlings that had carried away his chains), all screeching and fluttering to alight on a telephone wire. First they looked like a string of brown beads; then like chattering children, bobbing and balancing, lined up for the race of their lives; but Mum had said she would use the telephone. "I'll ring from Melbourne to see how you are, so don't go away."

There was an arrow in the sky and it pierced the balloon. It fell back to earth clanking like a chain.

That wonderful feeling of calm and contentment and excitement, of being able to do as he pleased and not as other people said, turned over inside him like a page that was gone.

He couldn't go to the forest because he had to stay home.

He couldn't dig a hole because he wasn't allowed to use the tools.

He couldn't climb on to the roof because it would take too long to get to the phone.

His mother's words, everyone's words, thudded

over the top of him like traffic on a wooden bridge.

That horrid little telephone; that green monster was going to sit there all day like a big fat ear. For as long as he watched it it would brood; for as long as he thought about it it would threaten; as soon as he turned his back it would leap up and down screeching, "Don't do this. Don't do that. Don't. Don't." Then an hour later it would ring again.

That was why Mum had left it till last; so he couldn't argue; so he couldn't talk back. "I'll ring you from Melbourne, so don't go away." It was a real, grown-up, dirty trick.

"It's not fair," he wailed, and in a flash of temper hurled a stone from the path straight down the drive and out through the arch of cherry-plum trees to frighten a whole day's growth out of Mamie van Senden.

Mamie was wearing blue jeans and a yellow shirt and golden hair like a polished brass helmet and was trotting bird-like along the road with a bag and a shopping list.

"Arr!" she shrieked and stopped dead, framed by the arch, and looked straight up the path, straight at John, then shrilled, "Did you do that, John Sumner? What'd you do that for? You half-witted or something?"

"No, I'm not. I didn't know you were coming."

"I'll bet you did."

"I did not."

"It's dangerous, throwing stones. I'll tell my mum you're throwing stones. If I'd been riding my horse it would have bolted; then I'd have been killed and they'd have hung you for murder or something."

"Serves you right for riding a horse. What do you want to be riding a horse along here for? You shouldn't ride one until you're big enough. You're too little."

"You're only jealous 'cos you can't ride one yourself."

"I can too. I can ride any horse I like. I can ride a brumby. I can ride a steer."

"You're a real nut!" Mamie shrilled, and was about to shout something else but choked it back. Mamie had been told she was not to tease John Sumner about things he couldn't do, nor was she to play with him at all if she could avoid it in any way. It would be awful if he hurt himself and she got the blame. So she tossed her head and blushed and ran off along the road.

John blushed, too, because Mamie was nice and he was sorry he had frightened her. He wished he could carry her bag home from school the way Percy Mullen carried Elspeth Winter's bag, but he didn't like to, because Mamie was little, only nine. One day when she was bigger he would invite Mamie to his birthday party and Mamie would come.

"Mamie," he called, not very loudly, but she didn't answer, even when he hurried down to the arch and called again. "Mamie van Senden!"

She was too far away, or didn't want to hear.

John sat under the arch on a white-painted stone. It was the Stone of Scone, though he didn't tell people about it because it was important that it should never be known that the Stone in Westminster Abbey was not the real one. Otherwise there'd be the devil to pay. Sometimes when he sat there he was King John and people passing by were scurvy barons hatching a plot to weaken the power of the throne. Sometimes he was the Archbishop of Canterbury having a rest between coronations because kings were dying so thick and fast he was plumb worn out from lifting crowns onto their heads.

Harry Hitchman came along on his bike, steering in curves round invisible obstacles. They were land-mines and Harry knew if he brushed one with a wheel there would be a disaster. If one exploded it would trigger off the lot and the life of every person in the street depended on him.

"Hi, Harry."

Harry went by, weaving expertly, concentrating ferociously.

Harry was as sure-footed as a mountain goat, even on a bicycle. He was also strong enough to hit a ball to the fence on the oval where the grown-ups played, and that took some doing for a twelve-year-old, though he wasn't very bright at school.

"Hi, Harry."

Harry was tall for his age. Harry could fight, too. Harry gave Sissy Parslow a terrible hiding one night after school. They had to take Sissy to the doctor to be stuck together again. It was murder, the kids said. John had been sad in a way but he loved Harry for it because Harry got into awful trouble and took all the blame himself. "If that Sissy Parslow takes a poke at you again," Harry had said to John, "I'll let him have it next time, good and proper."

"Hi, Harry."

But Harry weaved away dodging land-mines. John was always a bit shy where Harry was concerned. He didn't like to raise his voice. He didn't want Harry to think he was a clinging vine.

Mrs. Parslow drove by in her new Holden Premier. She was driving two hundred yards to the shops. (Main Street was the next road across.) She thought she was Lady Muck. The car was ivory and bronze with white sidewalls. Sissy sat in front with a smug look on his face, with his nose turned up and his eyes directed ahead. He thought he was Christmas but he was a creep. His three horrible sisters sat in the back. They thought they were Princess Anne and hoped the neighbours were watching.

"It beats me where these people get the money from," John's mother had said. "Fred Parslow must have won it in a raffle."

Dad had replied, "Don't be catty, dear. If we can run two cars, allow them one."

"But you're a man of importance. Fred Parslow's a two-bit clerk."

A little black ant carrying a big crumb came close to John's foot. He stopped every few inches to catch his breath, then heaved up his load and struggled on. In ten minutes he covered a yard. He was terrific. Then another little black ant hurried down to meet him. He dashed here and there in a state of high excitement but the first little ant stood beside his crumb with one foot raised in a threatening manner. "Put your filthy paws on my crumb," he screamed, "and I'll knock you into the middle of next week! Find a crumb of your own."

"Hi, Percy."

Percy Mullen had a yapping Australian terrier on a lead. It was scarcely 9:45 but Percy already looked as though he had been dragged through a bush by the hair of his head. Percy always looked like that. The terrier was only knee-high to a grasshopper but was pulling fiercely on the lead and dashing to and fro, making horrible choking sounds. Percy had his hands full. "You bloomin' little pest," he wailed, "what's wrong with you? Do you want to strangle yourself or somethin'?"

"Hi, Percy."

"Hi, John."

"Where you off to, Percy?"

"Search me," panted Percy, and stumbled after the terrier.

"I'll come with you, Percy,"

"Little crumb," Percy yelled at the terrier, "you'll never die of old age, that's for sure!"

"Hey! Percy!"

The call was like a little kid with short legs who couldn't catch up.

The street was empty again. Percy wasn't there. Sissy Parslow wasn't there. Harry wasn't there. Mamie wasn't there. Neither was the ant.

The Giffords' car went past.

Mr. Gifford was a shire councillor and most fearfully important. He came to the school on special occasions and spoke for half an hour. He was a fat man with white hair and purple cheeks and a nose like a heap of red gravel. He had a notice on his front fence, TRESPASSERS WILL BE SHOT. Kids used to walk by on the other side in case a cannon popped out. Mum said the notice had been there for thirty years, for as long as she had lived in Wilson Street, anyway. Mr. Gifford had never shot anyone—unless he buried all the bodies in secret or had come to a special agreement with Constable Baird about not getting arrested.

The grocer drove by.

"H-H-Hi, Mr. Neal."

Mr. Neal must have been busy doing mental arithmetic adding up his profits.

The Stone of Scone suddenly got too hard. It usually did after a while. Even kings when they got crowned didn't have to sit on it for hours.

"Aw, h-heck," John said, "I'd b-b-better do my blooming old model."

Then the explosion came.

Bang.

He felt like a billion bits blasting off in all directions.

"I'm not goin' back inside; I'm blooming well not."

He didn't know that his hand was beating his thigh, that he was stammering aloud.

"I'm going to do what I want to do. I'll—I'll build a tree-house. That's what I'll do."

The idea shocked him. It came so suddenly it could have dropped from the morning sky.

5
House in the Sky

John turned to run, but stumbled, and fell bewildered on the coarse gravel of the driveway.

He lay there stinging for several seconds before he moved (hurt more inside than outside), then discovered that he was trembling all over. "Oh, golly," he moaned, and shifted awkwardly to the grassy bank below the Stone of Scone. There, after a few tries, he managed with a shaking hand to dislodge the pieces of gravel that stuck to him. There was not much blood but he had skinned his kneecap and grazed an elbow.

"It's not fair. Other kids don't fall."

Mum would say, "How did it happen? How could you possibly fall and hurt yourself like that? Weren't you making your model? Weren't you doing your project? Weren't you taking your nap? That's not a fall from standing up. That's a fall from running."

Little by little he straightened his legs and tried to relax before the stupid old shakes had a chance to set in properly. He had got himself too excited; the grown-ups were always telling him not to, but what did they know about it? It was like telling a tree not to grow or a seed not to send up a shoot. And to make it worse he was at the roadside and everyone passing would see; old stickybeaks peering through curtains might spot him, even Mamie or Harry or Percy might come back, or creepy Sissy Parslow and his horrible sisters might leer at him from their car.

John pleaded with the shakes to go away. "Not today. Please."

A car was coming, too, just when he didn't want it, stopping and starting, with a door slamming, but the engine running all the time. It would have to be the baker and if the baker found him like this Mum would hear, she'd be told, and that would be the end of it; there would never be another day.

"I told you so," Mum would say; "didn't I tell you,

John? What on earth must people think of me? Leaving you all alone."

He crabbed along the grassy bank because if he stood up someone might see him; then when he was screened by the arch of cherry-plum trees he crawled into it a little way, but not too far because of the spikes on the branches. Perhaps he could have walked to the house, but he wasn't sure of himself, and for some reason it had become very important that not a soul should know. He didn't really worry about it over much at other times, but today it was a matter of pride. Today he wasn't the little spastic kid; today he was John Clement Sumner, the red-blooded boy who lived inside the one that shook and jerked and smudged his pages.

The baker's van came on and stopped at the culvert and John shrank farther from sight. The door slammed, heavy feet crunched on the gravel, then halted. "Ah! There you are, young Sumner."

John could have died. The bread-carter's face peered in at him. "If it's a game of hide-and-seek, boy, I think you're on the losing side. I'll leave the loaf here. Your legs are younger than mine." He crunched back down the drive to the van, and stopped, and called back in a tone that poised a question in midair, "Are you all right, young Sumner? What the deuce are you doing in there?"

John's heart began to thud wildly, but he feverishly shook his head and pressed a forefinger to his lips and hissed loudly to express a warning.

The bread-carter shrugged. "So, I'm spoiling a game?" he said. "Trust me," then deliberately paused again with one foot in the van. "Who are you hiding from? Where are the others?" He was not convinced, but suddenly pulled a face, took his seat, and slammed the door.

John listened to him drive on to the next house, and then the next, and didn't move until long after he had forgotten all about the baker. He could think of nothing but the shakes and the tree-house and "Don't do this and don't do that," and the balloon that would never be a balloon until someone cut it free.

He edged out of the cherry-plum trees and sat on the bank and was surprised to see the loaf there. And he was supposed to have ordered buns, but hadn't. Now Mum would want to know why.

"I forgot, Mum," he'd say.

"But why?"

"Golly, I don't know. I didn't think of it."

"Didn't think of your stomach? You must have been

up to something. Come on, out with it."

He loped across the lawn with the loaf under his arm but walked well, so well that he couldn't help but notice it.

"Maybe it's gone!"

He tossed the loaf onto a cane chair where Mum sometimes sat on sunny afternoons, then said out loud,

> *"Mary had a little lamb,*
> *its fleece was white as snow."*

He didn't stammer either, and that was a hard piece to say at any time. He kept it specially for difficult times to check up on himself when no one was about to overhear.

"I'm not going inside," he announced to the tree-tops. "No fear. I'm not dead yet, not on your life."

He strode round the side of the house with increasing confidence (it was terrific), then strode back again calling the beat: "Left, right, left, right. Lift your feet there."

He crossed the front of the house, bowing ironically to the loaf on the cane chair, then marched cockily down the far side.

"At the double now. One two, one two."

It was marvellous; he pranced with his knees lifting high like a soldier on the parade ground, then stopped at the foot of a peppermint gum, a tree thirty years old, huge, graceful, with the first branch fifteen feet from the ground; the sort of tree that every boy wanted to climb.

"If only I *could.*"

He looked up, and up, and up. From way up there, seventy feet, eighty feet up, he'd see for a mile. He'd look down on Sissy Parslow's house; down onto the ridge of Sissy Parslow's roof. He'd look down onto roads and gardens and unsuspecting people who would never dream that John Clement Sumner was way up there. He couldn't do it, could he?

"No . . ."

He lifted his knees again, "At the double there. One two, one two," and pranced across the garden to the oak tree. It was thirty years old (planted on the same day as the peppermint gum, thirty years ago) and the first branch was five feet from the ground.

He looked up into a mass of foliage, a network of boughs, twenty feet up, perhaps thirty feet to the very top. But the leaves were so thick he would never see out of them. The oak tree was a jungle but the peppermint gum was a bird.

"No slacking there. Knees up, lad. One two, one two."

Into the copse of silver birch trees. They were thirty years old, too, and the first branch was four feet from the ground and dozens of slender branches mounted higher and higher like the rungs of a ladder up and up to forty feet, until the trees bowed their heads to each other, but so delicate way up there, so languid in the wind that he would have to stop half-way before the trunk bent, before it bent and bent to his weight.

"Whoa, there. Whoa. Don't bend any more."

Halfway wasn't higher than the ridge of Sissy Parslow's roof.

He looked over to the peppermint gum.

"You're a beauty, you are."

He crept back to her shyly, perhaps a little guiltily.

"You're so beautiful," he said. "You're the Queen. A crown for the Queen. Gee willikens; wouldn't it be terrific, way up there?"

The first branch was only twelve feet from the ground; it wasn't fifteen feet at all.

With a bit of luck he could chuck up a rope and loop it over the bough. Then he could shin up, hand over hand. He shivered. Other boys could do it. Girls could climb. Even babies could climb. Percy Mullen shinned to the top of the flagpole in Main Street and swayed and sang, "Yo-ho-ho, and a bottle of rum!" Wouldn't it be terrific.

> *"Fifteen men on the dead man's chest—*
> *Yo-ho-ho, and a bottle of rum!"*

There was a house in the sky up there. There was a flagpole; a ship with a tall mast. A lighthouse. There was a tower. A chimney stack. There was a whole new world up there. There was a linesman swinging on a belt mending wires. There was a storm at sea, an eagle, a mountaineer on the Matterhorn. There was a pilot, a sky diver, an astronaut. Oh, golly; heaven was up there.

He'd say, "Hi-ya, bird. Hi-ya, cloud. Hi-ya, Mr. Sun."

He'd say, "Hi-ya, God. I'm knockin' on your door."

No; perhaps not that. You weren't cheeky to God. But he wasn't being cheeky, not really. The deep-down meaning was something extra special that God would understand if he was anything like the God Mum talked about.

He'd say, "Hi-ya, God. Here I am."

Any kid worth his salt could shin up a rope with his eyes shut.

6
Jacob's Ladder

There wasn't a rope in the shed or behind the fowl-house or in the laundry or even under the back verandah, where in moments of crisis things had been known to be pushed out of sight. There wasn't a rope at all except a single grey-weathered fragment with tattered ends tied to a branch of the apple tree. Dad must have loved that bit of rope or it would never have been there. It was a miracle he hadn't burnt it, buried it, or tossed it out with the garbage.

John trudged here and trudged there, up to the top of the garden where the tomatoes and the sweet corn grew, down the side fences where the climbing geraniums grew, getting more and more stewed up inside.

Rope was like rusty nails and old paint tins and broken window-glass; other people always had it lying around. But Dad wasn't other people. Dad was so neat and tidy it was enough to drive a fellow nuts.

"Never a blade of grass out of place." That's what people used to say about his garden. Other kid's dads played golf at weekends or listened to the races or went to the pub with their mates; Mr. Blooming Sumner worked like a galley-slave in his garden, and if it turned out wet it was the end of the world, like it was an earthquake or a tidal wave or a cyclone or something.

Other people kept their rubbish; Dad took his to the tip. Other people had bits of everything like old horse collars or broken bicycle frames or saucepans with holes in them stuck all over the place, but Dad spat sparks and brimstone if he saw a toffee paper blowing around. He did have rope, of course—because Dad was prepared for everything—but it was neatly coiled and carried in the luggage trunk of his car. He supplied Mum with a piece, too, for emergencies on the road, but it was in the trunk of *her* car. It was *infuriating*.

It was a beaut word that; infuriating! But it would be horribly hard to say out loud.

Of course he had known all along he wouldn't find any rope. He had known he wouldn't be able to toss it up to the branch anyway. And if he did manage to toss it up, how was he to tie it so it wouldn't slip? It wouldn't stop there just because he wanted it to. The whole idea was stupid from the start. Whoever heard of a little spastic kid like John Clement Sumner sittin' up a gum-tree?

It was a terrific tree. People who lived round about didn't take any notice of it because there were about a million others, but visitors up from town used to admire it. "That's a lovely gum-tree. It's got a nice shape. It's not skinny and straight like the ones in the forest or gnarled like the ones in the foothills."

There was always the garden hose, but how could a fellow lift it twelve feet into the air and loop it over the bough?

Twelve feet? Fifteen feet if it was an inch.

There was always the ladder. Yeh. Like there was always the Sydney Harbour Bridge.

But it was there just the same, on a rack under the back verandah. Dad pulled it out every June when he scraped the dead leaves out of the gutters and cleaned the chimneys. Then he pushed it back in again and said without fail, "Thank heaven that's over. I always feel nervous on a ladder. Next year I'll get someone in to do it."

It was a long ladder. It was a strong ladder. It was older than John himself, but still looked like new. It was painted red at the tips and the rest of it was varnished all over. It was almost as good as a fireman's ladder. It always looked terrific leaning against the house, just as though at any moment Dad would appear with a damsel in distress slung over his shoulder. Except that he usually appeared covered in soot from head to foot and swearing a treat. Not that John could hear the words, because Dad wasn't like that. But there he would squat, hanging on tooth and claw, muttering to himself.

John got his hands on the ladder and started dragging it out. It weighed about a ton and he had to heave like mad. It came out from under the house like a long, long tooth being dragged out by a sweating dentist. "It can't be any longer," the dentist said; "it must be coming up from his boots. Open the skylight, nurse. Bring me a ladder."

How would he ever push it in again?

The thought hit him just as the far end teetered

over the edge of the rack, pivoted sharply from his grasp, and whacked with a splitting sound to the ground.

He froze with eyes shut and fists clenched, hoping for the ladder to say, "I remain sound in wind and limb. What are you in a fizz about?" But the ladder said nothing, so John had to look for himself. There lay all fourteen feet of it prostrate on the grass, bruised a bit perhaps, aching a bit perhaps, but with not a break in sight.

For a few sweet moments the world was a happy place; then other matters returned to mind. "What am I cheering for? Mum's bound to know I've had it out, because how am I to lift it up to put it back in again? I've cooked me goose to a crisp. And how am I going to get it up against the tree, anyway? I couldn't get that dirty great ladder up to a tree for a hundred dollars, not for two hundred dollars even. I'm as silly as a wet hen."

He walked in a circle muttering like Dad at chimney-cleaning time, then stopped in his stride and regarded first the tree, then the ladder, and finally the rack under the verandah.

"It's a certain thing if I *can* get it up to the tree, liftin' it back onto the rack'll be a pushover."

So he dragged it across the lawn and placed the top rung against the bottom of the trunk, round the far side where no one could see from the house, then looked up, and up, and up.

"You're the king," he said, "a crown for the king."

No one would imagine that John Clement Sumner was way up there.

He'd see over into Main Street. He'd see people walking in and out of shops. He'd see the bus stop; people getting off the bus. He'd see the ridge of Sissy Parslow's roof way below. But he'd never be able to tell Sissy about it, because Sissy was a tattletale. Sissy wouldn't say to the kids, "Don't tell anyone, will you! Don't let the grown-ups know! John Sumner climbed that whoppin' big tree all on his own." That was not the way Sissy would do it. He'd tell his mother instead. Then Mrs. Parslow would tell. Then they'd all tell and soon Mum would hear about it. Then it would be nag, nag, nag, you'll never be left alone again, you naughty boy.

Living with people was awful.

When he grew up he'd buy an island and put a castle on it with a moat round it. Maybe a penthouse or something; castles were getting a bit old-fashioned. He'd stick a notice up on the beach, TRESPASSERS

WILL BE SHOT. He'd have a volcano or a bottomless pit to chuck all the bodies in. He'd have a swimming pool with deep water at both ends. He'd have a drawbridge and man-traps and a pet lion called Elsa. He'd have towers all over the place that a fellow could climb, and holes all over the place that'd fill up with water in winter. His wife would be Mamie. He'd have a lighthouse flashing a signal to warn ships away at night. The signal would read, "Get lost." Harry and Percy would visit him at Christmas but when Sissy Parslow came the lion would eat him.

He heaved the ladder up a couple of feet and jammed the top rung against the tree, leant on it, and panted.

He heaved again.

It was a surfboat and the engine wouldn't work and he had to row like crazy to get out to the rocks before Mamie was swept to sea.

"Heave!"

Maybe the ladder had arms like an octopus because somehow or other it was on top of him and he was underneath it and seas were breaking everywhere and that bloomin' tree was pushing the wrong way like something that wanted to fall down. Then he saw that it wasn't Mamie on the rocks but Sissy Parslow and that was the stone end of it. He wasn't busting his boiler for that creep.

So he flopped under the ladder, flat on his back, arms spread, his tongue almost hanging out, to float in the surf for a while, to toss round on the waves, but looking up at the tree from that angle made him giddy. The trouble was when he had a good look it really was Mamie out on the rocks.

"I'm comin'," he yelled. "Hang on."

He got his back under it.

"Heave. Heave ho."

Then he saw another surfboat on the way out and Percy was doing the rowing. "I'll save her," Percy said, "don't you worry, John."

John shook his fist. "Be blowed to you, Percy Mullen. You've got a girl of your own. You go and save *her*. Mamie's mine."

A surfboard came into view and Harry Hitchman was kneeling on it and driving it out through the waves with long, strong thrusts of his arms. "I'll save her," Harry said, "you'd better get back to shore."

"I will not go back to shore. Do you think I'm a sissy or somethin'? I don't need anyone to fight my battles for me. You'll see.

"Heave. Heave. Heave.

"I'm coming, Mamie. Hang on, Mamie.

"What do they want to make ladders so heavy for? The bloomin' thing must be solid iron.

"Come on, *heave*.

"You're real weak, John Clement Sumner. If you were a cup of tea they'd pour you down the sink."

He flopped on his back again among the fallen leaves, his chest heaving, sweat breaking out of him.

"Strike me, it's hot."

But the ladder still leant against the trunk and the top rung must have been seven or eight feet up. It was well on the way. Not real bad after all, and Percy had broken an oar and was helpless and Harry had been swamped. Harry had lost his board and was chasing it; it'd be up on the beach before he got to it. John Sumner might have been having a rest but he was the only one left in the race.

"Hang on, Mamie," he said, "I'm still coming."

He had the shakes in the knees again but they were a different sort of shakes and he murmured, to make sure, "Mary had a little lamb, its fleece was white as snow." It flowed off his tongue as though every word had just been oiled.

"Blurts to you, Mr. Robert Macleod," he said. "You don't know everything."

"*That* is a vulgarity, John. You'll not be common in this house."

"Blurts to everybody. Everybody gives me a pain. Do they think I'm a saint or something? Do they think I'm a bunch of flowers? Blooming projects and plastic models. You'll not save my girl, Harry Hitchman; I'll save her myself."

He lurched the ladder up another couple of feet, inches at a time, but it was getting heavier and heavier and harder to manage. It was harder than rowing any silly old surf boat. It was like a Scotsman tossing the caber. Maybe it was like doing a pole vault and getting stuck on top of the pole halfway over. Mamie was in a tower waving a white handkerchief. "Help. Help."

"Be blowed to you, Mamie van Senden. You got yourself into it; you get yourself out of it. You'll have to jump. I can't get way up there."

He sank back to the ground at the foot of the ladder, hot and shaking, with sweat in his eyes.

The telephone was ringing.

It sounded about half a mile away and was all mixed up with the thunder in his head. "Oh, golly," he panted, and reeled to his feet and stumbled up the steps on to the verandah.

"All right," he wailed, "I'm coming. I'm coming. Put a sock in it, will ya."

It was on a low table near the fireplace in the living room, screeching with impatience.

"John. *John.* Are you there, John?"

"Yeh, yeh. I'm here."

"What are you panting like that for?"

"Who's panting?"

"You were a long time answering. Didn't I tell you not to go away? That's why you're panting, isn't it? You've had to run."

"Gee, Mum, of course I had to run. I was up the garden."

"You know you are not to run. You should have walked."

"Then I'd have been later still. Then it'd have taken me longer to get to the phone."

"Has the baker been?"

"Yeh, Mum, yeh; he's been."

"Did you get your buns?"

"No . . ."

"Why not?"

"I forgot."

"Forgot your stomach? What've you been up to? You've been up to something, haven't you?"

"Gee whiz, Mum . . ."

"You haven't got that Percy Mullen boy with you, have you?"

"Of course I haven't."

"Well, who have you got?"

"*No one.*"

"Is it raining?"

"Raining? Of course it's not raining."

"It's raining in town. You haven't got yourself wet or anything?"

"The sun's shining, Mum. There isn't any rain."

"I've got your school trousers on the line, so you'd better bring them inside or I'll never get them dry."

"Golly, I said the sun's *shining*. You never listen to me, do you?"

"You've been up to something."

"No, Mum, *no.*"

There was a pause and he could hear her breathing down his neck. He could almost feel her breath like a breeze coming in puffs. She seemed to be beside him physically, questioning him, accusing him.

"Never again, John, if you've been up to anything; you know that, don't you? I'm trusting you."

That meant she wasn't.

"I've got to go now. I'll ring again at lunchtime. I'm having lunch with your father. Then we'll see Mr. Macleod together. Remember now, no hot drinks, no toast or anything. No messing about with the stove. Don't forget to take your nap."

Click.

The click was a lovely sound and he dropped the phone suddenly as if it had become a slimy thing wriggling in his hand, as though the touch of it made him sick.

After a while he drank two glasses of water and raided the biscuit barrel and sat outside on the verandah steps feeling lost and tearful, feeling as though someone had died.

The mynas were back in the clamshell, bathing at the deep end; the parrots were back in the apple tree, pirating fruit; the starlings were lined up in their millions all along the telephone wires thirty miles to town.

Kids were having a rough-house somewhere; he could hear the shouting in a distant sort of way. Percy Mullen's dogs were still barking their silly heads off. Harry Hitchman would be down at the oval hitting a ball to the fence. Sissy Parslow and his horrible sisters would be rushing from door to door telling tales. Mum would ring again at lunchtime.

That was the way his world went. The other world where kids did as they pleased was about a million miles away.

He cried inside himself for a few minutes, then wandered across to the ladder and sat on the bottom rung. It wasn't a comfortable seat and something moved him to try a somersault, but he made an absolute mess of it as usual and rolled onto his side. The postman's whistle blew somewhere, a forlorn, empty, lonely sound. He cried a bit more and ended up on his back looking at the sky. The sky was miles away; the top of the gum-tree was miles away. A hawk wheeled in the emptiness between. It was lonely up there, too, but different.

"Hi-ya, bird. Hi-ya, cloud. Hi-ya, Mr. Sun."

Saying it made him cry again and he hated crying, even when no one else was around.

A voice came to him from a long way off; one of those *imagined* voices. It sounded rather cross. "I didn't put myself up in this tower, you know. You did, John Sumner, with your stupid make-believe. You can't expect me to jump. I'll break my neck. You've got to come up to carry me down."

It was Mamie still waiting to be rescued, but John wasn't interested any more. "I can't climb that high," he said. "I can't get the ladder up."

"I bet Harry Hitchman would get the ladder up."

"Blow Harry Hitchman. Harry Hitchman gives me a pain."

"Save me, Harry. John Sumner can't get me down."

"You shut up, Mamie van Senden. It's not fair bringing Harry into it."

"I won't shut up. Save me, *Harreee!*"

"Harry can't hear you. He's gone away to do things of his own. I suppose you're going to go away, too, aren't you, Mamie van Senden?"

She went away.

Nothing was left but the sky and the gum-tree and the ladder.

"Why don't you go away, too?" he snarled at the ladder.

But the ladder was real and didn't have to go away.

"I'm going to do my model. It's got 227 pieces. When it's finished it'll be a yacht for putting on the shelf. Then I'll paint it white and take it to school and all the kids'll say it's terrific. But they'll know it's only 227 pieces out of a box."

He rolled over sideways, over and over downhill into the geraniums at the fence. "I hate geraniums. They stink." But he put up with the smell because he couldn't be bothered moving. He didn't care about anything. What was the use of caring? The answer to everything was either "don't" or "can't." There was only one John Clement Sumner and he was the one who shook and jerked and smudged his pages.

He squinted across the grass to the foot of the ladder, then up the ladder. The top was only about five feet from the bough, but might as well have been fifteen feet or fifty. He might as well have left it under the house and saved himself a lot of agony, because he still had to get it back in place just as though it had never been touched.

Perhaps if he asked Percy and Harry they'd help. They couldn't even *think* he was weak if it took three of them to get it back, but Harry would say, "I'll do it." Then Harry would pick it up by himself and do it. Then they'd say, "But what did you take it out for?" They wouldn't know that before he had asked for help he had dragged it all the way to the tree and back to the house again. "Aw, I don't know," he'd say, "just for fun, I suppose."

But it wasn't for fun. It was deadly serious. It was for something terrific that hadn't happened; like everything else that never happened and never would.

"I'm going to do my project. I'll cut some pictures out of *Women's Weekly* with my plastic scissors."

The ladder began to sneer at him. He wanted to rush it and give it a good kick, or push hard from the side so that it would fall with a crash. Several times the urge came like a command, but his body wouldn't move; it wanted only to lie on the ground.

"I wish you'd go away, you bloomin' old ladder."

But the ladder leant against the tree like a tough character in a film. The ladder spat a squirt of tobacco juice. "I'm stayin' right where I am, see. Are you makin' somethin' of it?"

"Oh, go away. You're only a ladder."

"I'm goin' no place, kid. I'm stickin' right where I am. No one pushes me around."

John edged off a yard or two from the geraniums; the smell of the leaves crushed by his own body was too strong.

"I wish I'd gone with Mum."

He sat up and clasped his legs and rocked miserably backwards and forwards, and for a moment remembered something of a long time ago: a curious and uneasy memory of perhaps a three-year-old sitting up in his cot, clasping his knees, rocking. For a moment there weren't any years between: he *was* little, he was that baby again; then the moment was gone.

"No!" he cried.

He felt hot and prickly and cruelly ashamed. His face twitched, his hands jerked, and on impulse he scrambled to his feet and rushed at the ladder. He grabbed it viciously near the bottom and wrenched it from the grass. By the top rung it shot up the trunk of the tree as though propelled and struck the bough.

It hit with a crack almost like a whip and jarred all the way to the ground; but it stayed there and did not fall down.

7

Open Road

Something happened to John. A storm passed through him. There was a battlefield and he was in the middle of it, flaying at heads in armour with a flat sword. There were screams and shouts and sour smells. It was savage.

Then there was absolutely nothing.

After a time he saw the ladder against the tree, butted up to the bough. It was a road to the sky and the road was open.

He was puzzled. He had not done it himself; of that he was sure. It was a miracle. He *could* not have done it. Lifted that dirty great ladder?

79

Numbed, he moved aside and sat back from it on the grass with legs crossed, not sure of himself, not sure of anything.

Oddly, the ladder did not break up rung by rung, did not melt like wax, did not disappear in a puff of smoke. It would not have surprised him if it had. But it was not a ladder that he had invented; it was not fashioned of substances he had imagined; nor was the miracle a feat of strength performed in a dazzling dream.

He had been so certain that this extraordinary event could not occur, but there stood the ladder ready for his use, as though it had never stood anywhere else. But his heartbeat was becoming a thud in his head and a breath-catching pulse in his throat. He was becoming frightened, and something inside him seemed to be falling endlessly. The longer he stared the more frantic his fall became, the faster his fears tumbled one over the other like dozens of people falling head over heels into an ever-deepening hole.

Then he looked up again to the long, slender curves of branches way up high like thin arms, to the topmost twigs like hands, to the last leaves groping like blind fingers for the sky, and there was a giddiness in him and a sickening wave of alarm. There was a cliff and he was on crutches at the edge of it.

He scarcely realized it any longer but he continued to shuffle away in nervous fits and starts, and all the things he should be doing were nagging at him, were noises that could not properly be heard: his model and its 227 pieces, his project and its pictures of cheeses, a library book half-read and worth finishing. Thousands of things; thousands of things he had to do; he could think only of three. But they were matters of urgency, they were immediate, and nothing else of any description was of any importance at all.

The noises became louder and louder, completely demanding, and he had to run to them, had to race across the lawn towards the house because that was where they were; the project, the model, the library book were all in the house shouting for attention behind doors and walls.

Then he stopped as though caught suddenly in his flight by a pair of strong arms, but nothing touched him; ahead of him was something that he saw. It was a girl.

She said, "Are you a nut or something?"

It was Mamie in blue jeans and a yellow shirt and golden hair like a bright helmet. She was eating an apple and drooped a bulging shopping bag to the ground by one handle. It was not the Mamie of the surf-drenched rocks or the Mamie of the tower, but the real Mamie who lived seven houses away on the right-hand side of Dawson Street, going up.

John stammered at her but it was a sound that meant nothing to himself or to Mamie either.

She took a bite from the apple. "Isn't your mum home?"

He shook his head.

"She'll shoot you when she comes home. You're awful dirty."

He was so breathless, so distressed, so ashamed. He was dust and grass and sweat and dirt from head to foot. He wouldn't have cared if he had dropped dead. He tried to speak, but couldn't, and realized that his hand was beating his thigh. It was a painful effort of will to stop it.

"I've been shopping," Mamie said. "Mum told me not to dawdle. But I did. She's going to be cross. Do you want a bite?"

He shook his head.

"I've eaten *two*." She rolled her eyes. "Mum'll scream. What are you doing?"

He tried to explain, but couldn't; tried to say that he was playing big-game hunting and was fleeing because his rifle had jammed, but it was a meaningless gabble.

Mamie began to look uncomfortable, began to wish she hadn't come—as she was supposed not to have done. She had wandered in only to dodge Mum for a while longer, but even putting up with Mum's performance when she came in late with two apples short, one cake gone, and three cents spent from the change would be better than this.

"I'd better be going," she said. "Mum'll scream."

"Don't go," he blurted out.

Mamie looked at her feet (she was just a bit frightened) and gathered up the stray handle of her shopping bag. "Got to," she said. "'Bye."

She skipped a little as she went, but not because she was happy. Mamie really wanted to run, and when she was round the side of the house, out of sight of John, she made no secret of it to herself and scuttled down the drive as fast as she could go. When she hit the road she looked back, but John wasn't behind her and she thanked her stars for that. "He's a real nut," she said. "He's a real crazy kid; they ought to stick him in a home."

John still stood where his scramble to the house had halted. He was furious, mad with himself, mad with Mamie, mad with the world. He wanted to break things, wanted to swear, wanted to jump up and down and stamp his feet. Never, never had he shaken to a fury like it. He was so ashamed, so burnt up with all the frustrations and prohibitions and failures and *don't do this*'s and *can't do that*'s of a whole lifetime that he was almost beside himself.

"You lousy, rotten ladder!" he screamed and started jerking about in circles and snatching at clods of dirt from the garden and hurling them at the tree.

"It's not fair, it's not fair. Other kids climb. Other kids don't make fools of themselves in front of their girls. You rotten old tree."

He rushed it and hit it with his fists. He kicked the tree. He swore at it. He grabbed at the ladder and not comprehending his actions all but ran up the rungs, stumbling, clawing, fumbling, until he was at least ten feet from the ground. There he stopped, suddenly shocked.

Everything went cold and became a mist.

So suddenly it happened; cold inside; cold outside; no fury left; no violence; not even any words.

The mist cleared and his legs somewhere below were trembling like reeds and his hands up above were clenched white about the side rails. He was stretched on the ladder, frozen in the act of a stride, like a victim of the torturer's wheel whose body was to be smashed when the wheel turned.

*   *   *

Cecil (Sissy) Parslow called to Mamie as she went by. He was leaning on his fence scratching his neck.

"What've you been up to, Mamie van Senden? What did you run out of the Sumners' place like that for?"

"He's a real nut," she said.

"Who is?"

"That John Sumner. He scared me stiff. He was fair frothing at the mouth. His mum's not home, either."

"He's on his *own?*" Cecil screeched.

"He said he was."

Cecil pulled a face. "You're a nut yourself. He couldn't have been having much of a turn if he spoke to you."

"I'm not a nut. You should've seen him. I just stood and watched. Better than a clown."

"He was havin' a turn and you didn't do anything?"

"He's having them all the time, isn't he? I was scared. Do you want a bite of my apple?"

"After you've been slobbering all over it? Not blooming likely."

Mamie sniffed and turned for home and threw the core into the bush.

Cecil Parslow headed for the Sumners' place. It was hostile territory, three vacant blocks away and over the road, so he stuck his thumbs through his belt and swaggered a bit but hurried because he had been told not to go away, that lunch would be early because Mum might drive down to Auntie Ellen's to show her the new car.

He was not sure why he was heading for the Sumners' or why the thought of John Sumner all on his own should worry him any. Maybe it was curiosity. The kid was a menace; being in the same class at school was bad enough; living in the same street was the real end. But he went just the same, at least until he got to the arch of cherry-plum trees. There he stopped, still with his thumbs defiantly through his belt, but with a distinctly uncomfortable feeling everywhere else.

He didn't like going into Sumners' place. It was an unfriendly house. It was too neat and tidy. He didn't mind John Sumner that much, not really, but every time he talked to him it ended in a row. John Sumner always called him "Sissy" but other kids called him Cecil or See-sal or Weasil. He didn't mind anything except Sissy. Every time he heard it he saw red. He had punched John Sumner one night after school for calling him "Sissy" and there'd been an awful fight with Harry Hitchman. It wasn't fair, because Harry was twice his size; Harry had arms like a kid of fifteen. And what did Harry care about John Sumner, anyway? He'd cross the street so he wouldn't have to talk to him. Same as all the kids. They all dodged him when they could, because he wasn't allowed to do this and wasn't allowed to do that and playing with him was like sitting in church. At least he, Cecil, never dodged away.

Mum said they shouldn't send John Sumner to an ordinary school because it wasn't fair on everybody else. Mum said he was like it because the family was too clever; too many brains never did anyone any good.

Dad said it was up to everybody to give the poor little devil a go; it wasn't his fault; they'd probably dropped him on his head when he was a baby or something.

The teacher said (when John was away sick) that the cerebral palsy condition was an accident of birth that could happen to anyone and children who weren't "spastic" should thank God in their prayers every now and then that it hadn't happened to them.

Percy Mullen said it was a bit of a drag having him tagging along like a lopsided shadow all the time, but he was harmless.

Auntie Ellen said it must be very trying living close to a handicapped child, always being reminded of it and everything.

Mamie van Senden said he was a nut.

Harry Hitchman said he had a terrible temper and screamed blue murder and broke things, because he had heard him at it from half a block away.

So Cecil stopped under the arch of cherry-plum trees and wanted to go farther but was not brave enough; even though Mrs. Sumner (who unnerved him somehow) was not there.

Perhaps for the first time he openly confessed to himself (*because* Mrs. Sumner was not there) that he wanted to be friends with John Sumner; for years and years, deep down, he had known there was a bond, that of all the kids only John Sumner would be his real mate, like soldiers together, like blood brothers, like partners against the world. But they always said the wrong things to each other, always pulled the wrong faces at each other, and Cecil would only get into trouble at home.

He slouched back up the street, scratching his neck, his defiant thumbs forgotten.

"Cecil! Where are you, Cecil? Lunch is ready."

8

Hi-ya, Bird

John panted rapidly through his teeth, and all the world was a gigantic ache, a terrible pain, and a continuing fright.

The sweat on his hands was like grease, and his fingers were slipping down those varnished rails a fraction of an inch at a time, in tiny jerks. Each jerk was a spasm of fear that he felt in his heart as though something there had ripped.

Sweat was running into his eyes and mouth; it was creeping in horrible streams from his armpits. It was strength dripping out of him, his life dripping away. His whole body was soft, was limp, was melting. His body was becoming longer and longer and heavier and heavier. It felt like an object made of Plasticine stretching on a hot day, an object that in the end had to tear or break or fall apart.

He tried to go up but couldn't. He pleaded with himself, commanded his body to climb, but nothing responded. His body could have been another person a mile away for all the attention it paid. It was like calling to Mum in the middle of the night when she was asleep and all the doors had slammed shut.

He bore down on his legs, he pushed, he heaved, but nothing was there, no strength and no feeling; he could have been dead down there in his legs for all the use they were. He clung on, held on, pleaded, prayed.

Nothing answered him; nothing from the inside; nothing from the outside. It was Mamie who had driven him up here but even Mamie was gone. Only the ground was down there; way, way down there. It was hard, that ground. It hadn't rained for a month. The thick roots of the gum-tree broke the surface and they were there, too, like rods of iron, like rails. It wasn't soft grass or deep grass. It was dry grass shaved to the surface by Dad's lawnmower. There was nothing down there to fall on; only things to break on; and that ghastly slipping away through his fingers went on and on, each jolt another drop of life gone.

There were not even splinters to bite into the flesh of his hands. The ladder was so smooth; rubbed smooth with sandpaper and varnished. That was Dad all over. Even his ladder was perfect. If he hadn't sanded it, hadn't varnished it, hadn't washed it clean after every use *it wouldn't have slipped through his fingers.*

There were weary voices inside him, arguing. One was stern (though tired) and the other desperate. One sounded something like Mum; the other sounded like part of himself.

"I didn't mean to climb the rotten thing in the first place. Never, ever. It was only pretending. All the time I wasn't going to do it. All the time it was only *pretending.*"

"It wasn't pretending."

"It was, it was. Like everything else it was only pretending."

"Getting the ladder down from the rack—was that pretending? Getting it up to the tree—was that pretending?"

"Of course it was. I'm not silly, I'm not crazy. I know I can't climb."

"Kicking the ladder. Punching it. Swearing at it.

Running away from it. Were they all pretending?"

"I don't know, I don't know."

"You got up here, didn't you? You climbed here. You couldn't have got here any other way. All the time you knew it was going to happen, but you knew that when you got here you'd fall."

"It's that rotten man telling me about the balloon."

"It was easy for him. It was nothing to him. He was only a stranger passing by."

"He had a nice face and had a nice voice. I think he was handicapped, too. I *believed* him. I'm sorry I said he was a rotten man."

"He was a stranger. He didn't understand. He didn't know."

"He did know."

"If he knew, you wouldn't be hanging here now; you'd be climbing up and up and up. You'd be saying hi-ya, bird; hi-ya, cloud; hi-ya, Mr. Sun. You'd be way up there looking down on Sissy Parslow's roof and on Main Street and on people getting off the bus."

A whimper broke out that he had striven to hold back and with the whimper came the shakes; they came together: shakes that he could feel even in the ladder. It shook under him, throbbed under him, and nothing was left in his hands, nothing at all. They stayed there, still slipping, still sliding, but numb.

He would lie down there, perhaps broken, perhaps dead, and no one would know. People coming to the back door wouldn't see him; Mum coming home wouldn't see him; because the ladder was hidden from the house. Mamie had faced the tree but had never guessed that the ladder was there.

Mum would call, "John. Where are you, darling?" And she would become more frantic; she would dash here and dash there crying out; and then after a while she would find him. "Oh, John. I knew all the time I should never have left you. All these years I have kept you safe. In one day you kill yourself."

Even now if he yelled (if there was breath enough) would anyone hear? Would they take notice? Would they come? Would they understand if they found him, not on the ground, but still crabbed grotesquely on the ladder? Would they understand why he had done it or would they say in scathing grown-up tones, "Silly little fool. Stupid child. Idiot. Get down from there"?

"I can't."

"If you can get up you can get down."

"I can't."

"Come on down at once, John Sumner."

"It's no use. I can't go up and I can't get down and I can't even fall."

He flowed like fluid into the crevices of the ladder,

and hung there by the crook of an arm, by a knee bent through the rungs, and by his chin. He became hooked by the chin, his head went back, and he strained against something solid—himself—his own body fighting and crying to prevent its strangulation. There were no shakes, not now, only a war to the death against a rung of wood and his own weight.

He was not going to fall, not going to die on the ground; he was going to choke on the ladder and they would find him there strung up like a chicken. The flag was at half-mast and kids at school would say, "Did you hear about that stupid John Sumner? Couldn't even climb a ladder."

He screamed with indignation deep inside and not a sound came out, but his body of jelly turned into muscles and sinews and bones. His hands and arms moved, his legs moved, he fought off the pressure at his throat and raised himself up. He raised himself up three excruciating steps and with clawing fingers touched the bough.

He wanted to let go, to hit the ground in a heap, simply to know that it was over, but his fingernails were clawing bark and he could see this thing happening as though he stood a short distance off and something started cheering like thousands of people.

"That's the boy, John. Stick at it, John. You'll show 'em, John. Keep going, John. Don't stop now, John."

"I can't. I can't."

"You'll do it, John. It's a long way down but a short way up."

"It's *impossible.*"

"There goes the balloon. Chase that balloon, John. Fight for it, John. After it, after it."

He fought to hold the moment and keep the mood and thousands cheered. He clawed and snatched and swung and madly scrambled and suddenly was crying. He was weeping as he had never wept in his life.

Only women and girls wept for joy; that was what people said; but it was not true. Boys wept like it, too.

He was sitting on the bough.

He couldn't see for tears, couldn't think, couldn't reason, couldn't look ahead or look back, but he knew what he had done.

"Hi-ya, bird. Hi-ya, cloud. Hi-ya, Mr. Sun. Here I am."

9
Ahoy!

Oh, the sky was a million miles deep with the flush of roses in it and he was there. He was singing in the sky:

> *"Fifteen men on the dead man's chest—*
> *Yo-ho-ho, and a bottle of rum!"*

The earth was way down below where gloom and misery were, and it could bally well stay there.

He tore at his shoe laces, wrenched off his shoes, and let them fall. They lay on the grass like cocoons cast off by butterflies with bright new wings.

He peeled off his socks soaked with the sweat of terror and let them fall also. They lay like crumpled masks of sorrow thrown away by laughter.

He sang in the sky, "Hi there, everybody."

He wriggled up the bough and reached for the next and pulled himself onto it. He went up and over it and straddled it like a horseman, flexing his toes.

"Hi there, everybody; I'm up in the tree."

Every cell of his body sang in the sky, "Yo-ho-ho. Yo-ho-ho."

He wriggled higher again and tore off flakes of bark and flung them through the leaves with a sound like waterfalls. He stuck a green twig between his teeth and chewed on the sap. It was nectar, sweeter than honey; sap that flowed in the sky. He patted the bough. "Giddee-ap there, bough." He sang to the sky and cared not at all that the sun wasn't there and the birds had flown away and the world above was heavy and grey. The rain-splashes in his upturned face were an exhilaration; were cool oil to anoint the king of the castle. "I'm the king; and all below are dirty rascals."

He went on with his hands out before him, reaching up, pulling up, and he wasn't the little spastic kid any more; he was the red-blooded boy that everyone had stifled; had said wasn't there.

"Yo-ho-ho."

He was an eagle, a mountaineer. He was Hillary scaling Everest. Rain was in his hair.

"Do you see me, Mamie van Senden? Hi there, Mamie on the ground.

"Do you see me, Harry Hitchman?

"Hi there, Percy Mullen. Who's up the flag-pole now?"

He was a steeplejack with nerves of iron.

"Do you see me, Mum?

"Do you see me, Dad?

"Do you see me, Auntie Vi? Blurts to your egg-flips to make me strong."

"Blurts to you, Mr. Robert Macleod. You'd cut a fellow open just to stitch him up again."

He was a monkey swinging by his tail.

"Blurts to you, Sissy Parslow, under your roof with the rain beating on it.

"Do you see me, Mr. Balloon? I wished for the treetops and here I am.

"Hi-ya, Main Street over there. Hi-ya, Mr. Butcher. Hi-ya, Mr. Baker. Hi-ya, rain; I'm coming up to pull you down."

He went up singing:

> *"Fifteen men on the dead man's chest—*
> *Yo-ho-ho, and a bottle of rum!"*

He struck a pose and raised an arm and declared

to the wide world, "Go play with your dogs, Percy Mullen." And added, "Go play with your ball, Harry Hitchman." And capped it stridently, "Stick your nose outside, Sissy Parslow, and I'll black your eyes."

Impulsively, he hugged the bough at his face, wrapped his arms about it like a warm friend. "You'll be my tree for ever and ever. I'll kill anyone who chops you down."

He was fifty feet in the air. It was a long, long way to the ground. He couldn't see the ladder any more, couldn't see the drag marks he had made across the lawn; saw only leaves and branches and rooftops gleaming wet, only the things of the air. Television antennae, power lines, telephone wires, chimney pots, street lights on poles, and rain.

"Oh boy, oh boy. Let it rain. What do I care?"

It was a sailing ship and he was in the rigging and there was a storm on the sea. He stood on a spar and shouted to the wind, "Ahoy there. Ahoy."

There were people on Main Street sheltering from the rain under shop verandahs. "Ahoy there."

Harry Hitchman pedalled past heading for home. "Ahoy there. Ahoy."

He wanted someone to know but no one heard. (They'd say: "Who's that up the tree? Not the Sumner boy? Oh dear, no. John Clement Sumner plays only with toys. That will be Percy, the youngest of the Mullen tribe.")

"Ahoy there. Can't anyone hear that it's me? Hey, Mr. Grocer. Hey, Mr. Butcher, way over there. Ahoy."

But no one heard and no one saw.

It would come to Friday's news session at school: "Percy Mullen, what did you do while school was in recess?"

"Dug lots of beaut holes, Miss."

"Harry Hitchman, what did you do?"

"Hit lots of balls to the fence, Miss."

"John Sumner, what did you do?"

"Climbed a gum-tree, Miss."

"This is news time, John Sumner, when we speak only the truth."

"But I did, Miss. I climbed fifty feet high, all on my own in the rain, Miss."

"You disappoint me, John Sumner. I thought you were a truthful child. I will ask again and I expect an honest reply."

How could anyone believe when no one had heard and no one had seen?

"I did my project, Miss. I made my model. I read

my library book. I sat in the window and watched the rain."

"Of course you did, John. But you should have said it in the first place. Why tell a lie?"

Would it come to that? Would he have to tell an upside-down lie because no one believed the truth?

"Ahoy! Ahoy! Ahoy!" There was command and demand and shrillness in his throat. "This is John Clement Sumner up a gum-tree. Hey, you deaf people on Main Street over there. It's me. You've got to see. You've got to hear."

But they stood under shelter with shopping baskets and baby carriages and bicycles and impatience in the greyness while the rain streamed down.

"Hey, Sissy Parslow, wash out your ears. It's me. Fifty feet from the ground. Maybe a hundred feet even. I won't black your eyes, Sissy Parslow, if you stick your nose out the door. Hey, Mamie van Senden; surely you can hear?"

He couldn't stop up here forever in the wind and the rain; he'd be catching a chill or going down with the flu. What was wrong with everybody? "Hey, you lot of stinkers, *it's John Clement Sumner yellin' up a tree.*"

They couldn't see him for leaves, they couldn't see

him for boughs. It was like looking out through the window of a darkened house. People in the street were plainly in view, but the person inside was shadowed in gloom.

He shuffled out farther until part of the oak tree came underneath and concealed the ground. He held on with thighs and arms and hands, even with his chest, and wriggled on into an intoxicating country where boughs swayed and branches were leaner and shelter from the rain was less. There he rode it like a polo pony, like a royal prince, his knees pressed in, head and shoulders back, and hands locked round the stub of a vertical branch.

It was everything he had longed for and never known. All words fled away, all demands that others should see him meant nothing any more. The bough swayed and he swayed with it; wind was like a cool sea against him; motion and wind together were a great calm that healed every pain he had ever known.

He was strong. He was free. He was a boy like any other boy.

The world came back again; the wind that was cold, the rain, the clothing that clung to him drenched through and through, the oak tree wet and stirring and separate underneath, and Main Street over there.

Nothing snapped back into view; it grew, and slowly became real; even the shopkeepers out on the open road, with the rain streaming down, pointing towards the gum-tree.

"That's the Sumners' tree. That's the Sumners' place. It's that boy. God, he'll be killed."

But of those things it was John who didn't hear.

10

The King

It was strange; he had tried so hard to attract attention, but when it happened he might even have been slightly sorry that his joy was not personal and private any longer.

Soon everyone would be saying, "Did you hear about John Clement Sumner?"

"The lad did it, to be sure. Everyone saw."

"John climbed up *there*?"

"You're terrific, John, the things you can do."

Of course he didn't care if the whole world knew.

He waved. "Ahoy, over there. It's me. You bet your boots it's me."

But they were turning to each other as though confused and more were stepping out from shelter onto the road. A man in a grey dust-coat stopped a passing car, another on a bicycle rode towards a side street that headed John's way. Boys started running, ignoring cries from their mothers to keep out of the rain. A motorcar horn sounded a series of short blasts.

"That fuss *can't* be for me."

But people were still pointing towards the tree as others joined them in the road; and coming up from his own house below, out of the chimney pot, was the clamorous ringing of the telephone.

John sat rigidly on his bough, swaying to the wind, dripping with rain, questioning the sanity of the world. "Surely not for me? I only wanted them to wave; only wanted them to know."

He started edging back from the extremity of his bough, embarrassed by it all. "Kids are always climbing trees. They can see kids up trees anytime."

The telephone stopped for a few seconds' pause and started ringing again.

"Strike me," John panted, "maybe it's Mum on the phone," and hastened his retreat along the bough, but it was only inches at a time.

He heard a car hit the culvert hard at the arch of cherry-plum trees, bottoming its springs, then it roared up the drive. He heard car doors slam, heard heels across concrete, and someone calling out loud.

"Are you all right, lad?" It was a man.

Then more voices of different kinds, some directed into the air, some urgently to each other: "Can you see him?"

"Where's his mother?"

"Mrs. Sumner, are you there?"

"Has he fallen? It's a wonder he held on at all."

Fists were hammering against the door and the telephone fell silent.

"There's a ladder over here. She couldn't possibly know. Good Lord, the poor woman will die."

John shuffled backwards as fast as he could move. He wanted to get to the trunk, to reach the way down, but there was a limit to speed on a swaying bough. They'd got it all wrong. They had thought he was in trouble, calling for aid. There were cars pulling up in the street outside; one was pale blue with a flashing light on top.

"His mother's not here. Try the houses round about. She might be having a cup of tea next door."

"I'm hanged if I can see him. He must have shifted in from that bough."

"It's a sticky one, Constable. He's terribly high and doesn't say a word."

"Golly," John moaned. "There'll be the devil to pay."

"Are you sure his mother's not about?"

"Her car's gone. I thought she never left the child."

"She doesn't either. She's marvellous. He's never left alone."

"Hey, young John. Let's hear your voice, lad. Give us a call."

"He's probably had a turn. He was easily sixty feet high."

"If he'd had a turn he'd be flat on the ground."

"Or caught up in a fork somewhere. Whatever possessed the child?"

"I see him. To the right. Over here. Higher than that. There!"

John saw the congregation far below, the upraised arms and pointing fingers. They were miles away, so unnatural and small. That couldn't have been the ground way down there, ridged with roots, and shaved with Dad's lawnmower. Their voices seemed so close (was it a trick of the rain?) but their faces were part of another world, like faces seen across an abyss, or suddenly through telescopes peering back at him from a distant planet. He began to turn cold; his grip tightened on the bough, and desperately he looked up, looked straight up, and called, "Please, please go away."

"He's panicked, all right. He's frozen, poor kid."

"I haven't panicked. Please, please go away."

"What did he say? Speak up, lad. We can't hear a word."

"*Go away.*"

"We'll certainly not do that."

"Are we frightening him, Constable?"

"*Frightening* him? He doesn't need frightening by us!"

"How did he get up there?"

"Climbed; climbed. What other way!"

"But he's almost a cripple."

"No cripple could get up there. Nor any man either in his right mind. I can't see a man swinging on that bough."

Half a dozen voices were running one over the other.

"If we get to him how will we hold him? If there's a struggle something will break and then the lot'll come down."

"I'll get myself down, if only you'll go and leave me alone."

"Can't hear a word he says. Look, boy, speak clearly, louder. Use your lungs. The wind blows your voice away."

"I think we're frightening him."

"If you go away I'll come down!"

"And what'll happen then? One slip and he'll be smeared all over the ground."

There was a boy's voice, shrill, as though weary of being ignored: "He's all right, Constable Baird. He's not stammering or anything."

"Are you an expert on these things, boy?"

"Gee, I live across the road—"

"I know where you live, young Parslow."

"I go to school with him an' everything. He always stammers when he's having a turn."

"That's so, Constable. John's not stammering. There's no panic up there."

"I *do* know the boy myself, Councillor Gifford; I have had considerably more to do with him than most. I would suggest, respectfully, that this is not the moment for amateur psychology, no matter how well informed."

"I beg to differ. We're dealing with a highly emotional child."

"Oh, for pity's sake, show me a child that isn't. I

wish everybody would go away and leave me to it."

"If we use our heads, Constable, applying this psychology you so roundly scorn, we'll have him down in no time."

"And I'm sure if everybody would shut up I'd be able to get on with the job! You're getting me rattled."

"*Oh, g-go away.*"

"What did he say?"

"He's *stammering*, Constable, and I am not in the least surprised."

"I know he's stammering; I've got ears of my own. Be of some use to me, somebody; you, young Parslow; there's rope in the car! Who's his doctor? What's his name?"

"It's some fellow in town."

"I know it's some fellow in town but *what's* his name? Doesn't *anyone* know? You, Bill Neal; scoot into the house and ring Doctor Jones."

"What can Jonesy do?"

"Nothing, I guess, unless the boy falls."

"Constable, he can hear every word we say."

"Whose fault's that, then? Mine? Where's the rope? Where's young Parslow? He's slower than a snail. Do go away, little girl. I know you only want to help, but please go away."

THE KING

"Talking here like this is absurd. We're frightening the life out of the child."

"Oh, for heaven's sake, Councillor. I'm the one who's got to climb the tree, not you."

Voices went round and round; words struck at John like a flail. He had never done anything that words hadn't spoiled. "Don't do this. You can't do that. Come away. Don't go there. No, no, no. You're different from other boys."

He couldn't even climb a tree without everyone going mad. They'd spoilt it now. It was as sour as anything had ever been. Worse, because it had promised so much more. Worse, because they were talking and he could hear. Other times they talked— of course they talked and of course he knew—but then he didn't hear and not hearing was as good as not knowing. Oh, he wished they'd go away or he'd fall.

The telephone rang, blaring up the chimney pot. There were shouts and calls and the voices of children he knew. Sissy Parslow was there. Harry Hitchman was there. Percy Mullen was there. Mamie van Senden was there. Oh, the shame. There were cars and trucks and vans. People were crowding in from both ends of the street.

, "Go away. I could have got down if you'd all stayed away. I'll never get down if you don't go away. Oh please, God, make them go away."

"John Sumner!"

It was a calm voice that he heard, much calmer than when the same voice had been on the ground. He had hated that voice down there; it had been a rasp with jagged teeth sawing across his nerves. It wasn't on the ground now. There were few sounds on the ground at all: the clamour had become indistinct as though someone had shut a door.

"Do you hear me, John Sumner?"

But John lay along his bough with his legs clamped about it and his arms clamped about it while it swayed. He couldn't answer; it would have been silly to have tried. He would have stammered and shaken all the more.

"John . . ."

The voice was still calm and quietly spoken. It penetrated. There was an authority in it that expected a reply.

"Can you hear me, John Sumner? Please let me know."

Now it was an order but John knew what stammering might do and let the order go on past him into the sky.

"John . . ."

He moved his hands on the bough and sat up. The giddiness was gone.

"Yes, Constable Baird."

"I'm on my way up. No harm can come to you if you do as I say. Can you see me?"

"I don't want to look."

"Very well then. Sit still and wait. You understand that I'm climbing, that I'm coming up?"

"Yes, sir."

John listened and heard the scuffling on the tree.

"What will you do when you get here?"

There was a pause. "Take you down."

"How?"

"We'll worry about that when the time comes."

"But you can't come out along my bough. I heard you say so. It'll break."

"I'll cross that bridge when I get to it."

It was quiet below and oddly he wasn't sorry about Constable Baird. His voice on the ground had been irritable (perhaps it had been afraid); but in the tree it was gentle and kind.

"It's a beautiful tree, sir."

"It is that, lad, but not made for climbing by old men like me."

"You're not old."

"Thank you, lad."

The voice was nearer.

"You've got your boots on, Constable Baird?"

"Yes; yes, I have."

"You'd do better if you took them off."

"Would I?"

"I took mine off. Do take yours off, please. I'd hate you to fall while you were climbing my tree."

"I'd hate to fall, too, but I was climbing trees before you were born."

"When were you born?"

After a pause: "1923."

"My dad was born before that. Mum, too."

A grunt as though of pain came from below.

"I can see you now, Constable Baird."

"Good boy, and I can see you."

The policeman was standing awkwardly with his right foot lodged in the crease of a bough where it sprang from the trunk of the tree. He had a coil of rope hooked through his belt and wore no tie or cap and his hair was wet in strands against his cheeks. He made no movement except that his chest heaved continually. His mouth was straight and beads of sweat on his face were mixed up with rain. (He was so nervous that he feared the boy would know.)

John said, "Where has everybody gone?"

"Away. You asked for them to be sent away."

"How far have they gone?"

"I don't know, but far enough away not to see or hear."

"You can't come any higher, can you?"

The policeman's lips were parted but his teeth were together. He seemed to be speaking through jaws that were closed. "How did you get up there?"

"Climbed along the bough you're on, then onto the next, then the next, then to here."

"I don't believe it. Someone dropped you by parachute."

"You can't come any higher, can you?"

The policeman shook his head. "I guess a boy can go where a man can't. I'm licked, John. You're the king."

"Am I, sir?"

"Indeed you are. You've done a remarkable thing."

"Thank you, sir."

"You're not afraid any more?"

"No, sir."

"Why? Because the people have gone away?"

"Yes; and because you're not cross with me any more. Because you haven't growled at me since you came up the tree."

The policeman wasn't angry, but he was afraid.

"Why did you do it?"

"To say 'Hi-ya, Mr. Sun.' I said it, too."

The man dropped his eyes. "Was it worth it, lad?"

"My word it was."

"But now we've got to get you down, to say 'Hi-ya, Mr. Ground,' and there's only one route that I can think of. An extension ladder like the firemen use, but how we're going to drive one in here I'm hanged if I know. Why couldn't you have picked a tree in the road?"

"It had to be this one, sir, where no one could see."

The policeman shook his head. "I'll work that out at a later date. Can you hang on for half an hour?"

"No, sir."

"You *can't!*" It sickened the policeman to think of the ground below.

"It's not that I can't, sir; I don't want to. If you go away and promise not to look I'll get down on my own."

"That's not fair, John. I can't do that. It's my responsibility to make sure you're safe."

"Why?"

"Because it is. It's the sort of thing that happens to policemen all the time. Another boy? Some little devil doing it for kicks; perhaps I'd leave him to it; but when he got down I'd thrash him round the block."

"Are you going to thrash me round the block?"

"No, John. . . . You're a very special case."

"Because I'm spastic?"

The policeman sighed. "Yes and no. It's more than that. You're the only boy I've ever met who climbed a tree to the sun—on a rainy day."

"It wasn't rainy when I started out. I'm not silly."

"I didn't mean it that way."

"I said, 'Hi-ya, bird; hi-ya, cloud; and hi-ya, God,' too."

"Did you, John?" (The boy himself was like some sort of god up there, like some sort of judge over the fears of a man.) "I think I've got to stay here, John. I'll arrange for a ladder. Who knows? I might need it myself to get down."

"Please don't get a ladder, sir. I don't want it, not at all. Just shut your eyes and let me try."

"No! You're not to do it!" His voice was so suddenly thin that John noticed it, with surprise. "If you put your mind to it you could wait up there for half a day."

"I'm not going to, sir."

"You must."

"Please, sir, please."

"*Look here!*" The thinness of his voice made him sound like a woman. "You do as I say, you little devil. I'm risking my life for you."

There was a sudden spasm through John, of dismay, almost of terror, and the policeman heard his cry. It was a cry that made the man bite on his lips with a hatred of himself that should have drawn blood, but already he was tugging openly at his imprisoned foot (it was too late to backtrack), the sole of the boot twisted and jammed in the tree that he dared not nor could not bend down to release. "Hey, you down there!" he yelled, with a shrillness unlike a man.

They came out from behind the tree on the blind side, and from under the oak. In seconds they stared up, a dozen or more.

"I want the Rescue Squad and I want them quick. There's nothing straightforward here."

Those people had been there all the time, hiding. Every word uttered they must have heard. The policeman had lied.

"No one else is to come up. It's too dangerous in the wet. It's bad enough for me. I won't accept the risk for another person. No one's blood on my head."

John clasped the bough to his chest and sobbed. Oh, that so much could go wrong with a beautiful day.

"And get on to his parents. For heaven's sake, make the effort to get them home."

11

Anybody Can Climb a Tree

John looked down into a swaying pool of grey and green and brown. Everything swam as though a window streaming with rain interrupted his view. Drowning there, it seemed, struggling upright in that curious pool, Constable Baird occupied the crease of the bough. The policeman was miserable and remorseful; he was silent, he was distinctly not at ease, and his leg was tiring and torturing him with its pain; not broken, not sprained: simply twisted against its natural way and securely held as though nailed. The lines of his face were drawn, sharply defined, shadowed with grey. He tugged, he twisted like a gaffed

120

fish. Why didn't he tell them on the ground?

John closed his eyes on it (still hugging his bough), then looked the other way. Main Street over there was like a river, like houseboats on a tidal stream. Everything swaying, everything swinging to and fro, everything wet, everything grey, traffic speeding up and down with wakes spraying from tyres hissing on the road, a red bus like a liner steaming into town. Rooftops like decks washed by the sea, treetops like rocks and breaking waves. Wind was like surf, rain was like spume; John was drowning, too.

His inner voice said: "It's a terrible thing I've done. I've involved the whole town. They're all waiting for me to fall. They're all thinking that I'm soft in the head. They always talk to me as if I was six, not twelve. They'll never understand."

Down there in that swaying pool of colours without names, straight down where sky met the ground, were grey faces in circles with blankets held taut between, were scores of cushions a yard high in the wet, and mattresses from beds stacked in a curve, and bent above them, bent in pain, was the policeman in the crease of the bough. Why didn't he tell them on the ground?

"Am I going to die? It's a sixty-foot drop with

boughs and branches as hard as axe blades in the way. But are they really in the way? Aren't they a ladder that I can go down?

"Do the people really have to go away? Does it matter if Constable Baird told lies? Does it matter if he says I'm not to try? That's what they always say. Don't do this. Don't do that. If I got up I can get down."

But the eyes of the man were like a fence of barbed wire. "You stay where you are, John Clement Sumner." They almost spoke it out loud. But the man was bending just the same. He looked like something breaking; with one arm round the trunk of the tree and his foot caught in the trap of the bough. If he had taken his boots off as John had said it wouldn't have happened to him at all. Was he too stupid or too proud to tell them on the ground?

A voice called from below. "Everything's fixed. The Rescue Squad's coming from Melbourne. It's only a matter of time."

"How much time?" asked Constable Baird.

"An hour."

"That's fine."

No one could see his foot from below. They were just as stupid down there not to have known. They didn't know that he was snared; that he was like a rabbit with a hind paw held in jaws of iron.

"His parents. Did you get them?"

"They rang from town and didn't seem surprised. Mrs. said she knew. Said she felt it in her bones. If she felt it in her bones why did she leave him behind? They're coming as fast as they can. How's the boy?"

The policeman looked up again, searching for John's eyes. "I don't know."

"Can't you tie him to the bough?"

"I'm not a bird."

"Throw him the rope and he can do it for himself."

"He'd fall trying to catch it. Use your brains. He's too high."

"There's a lad here who says he'll take it. If it's too thin up there for you, why not give it to a boy?"

"No one tries."

"Why not?"

"I said *no.*"

"You're too blamed stubborn for words. There's a boy down here pleading to try."

"Be a sport, Constable Baird. John's a mate of mine." It was Sissy Parslow.

"NO!"

"Please, Constable."

"Will you shut up, the lot of you! Go away!"

Then John found the policeman's eyes and something in them had changed. It *was* that crowd below that made it so hard, but the crowd would not go. Crowds were not made that way. But the order in the policeman's eyes was the same: "Don't move. Don't try."

John clung to the bough while it bent, while it swayed to the wind, while the policeman fought him with his eyes. "No, no, no."

He said *no* to everybody while he bent to the limit of pain.

"You're stupid," John said, but not out loud. "I reckon grown-ups are sillier than kids. I'm going down, anyway. I want to get down on my own."

"No," said the policeman with his eyes.

"Everyone always says *no* to John Clement Sumner. It's a habit; they can't help themselves. I got up here, didn't I? I'll get down."

He knew it was going to happen because his blood was running faster. In his mind he was already half-way down. He could feel himself going down even though he still clung to the bough.

"Don't you dare!" said the policeman with his eyes.

"Blurts to you, Constable Baird." Said secretly, inside.

What if he did fall? What did it matter?

John slid over his bough and hung from the armpits.

"Get back up there!" the policeman screamed.

John groped with his feet for the branch below. It was like walking in the dark away from the road, or pedalling a bicycle that wasn't there.

"Get up again! Pull yourself up again! For heaven's sake, boy, what are you doing?"

"He's slipped!" someone shrieked from the ground.

"He's having a turn."

"Watch him, watch him."

"Get to him, Constable. You've got to try."

The branch wasn't there. John's feet couldn't find it.

"You must go back, John. Anybody can climb a tree. It's the getting down that's tough."

John pedalled his feet into emptiness. *Anybody can climb a tree: it's the getting down that's tough.* It was a dirty thing to say. If Constable Baird had struck him he couldn't have hurt more.

John couldn't leg up again, back onto that bough; it was a question of strength that was nowhere in him. But the branch beneath had to be somewhere; perhaps across to one side. So he swung for it and brushed it with his toes. That had nothing to do with strength, only nerve, and he wasn't afraid. In a funny sort of way he wasn't even there.

"Blurts to you," he hissed, "I'm coming down."

"No, John!"

He swung again, knowing where to reach, and caught the branch between his feet and held on, panting, with his eyes closed.

"Get to him, Constable. For pity's sake try."

"*Shut up!*"

John shortened his stretch, sliding down little by little, bark like gravel grating across his skin, and hung by forearms and wrists like a mantis praying; part of him terrified, part of him fearless.

From nowhere came a human sound, only rain on leaves, only rain on roofs, only wind. Even traffic on Main Street made no sound.

He let go, pushing off like a boatman and fell clawing into foliage. He bounced like a ball, the branch creaking and writhing as though seeking to throw him off, but John clung on tooth and claw. Every button ripped away from his shirt; he had leaves in his mouth, bark in his hands, but he didn't fall.

Something sang in him: a wild elation, a furious defiance.

"Ahoy, there. Ahoy!"

He saw the policeman and, deliberately, mocked him full face. The man was ashen. John launched himself in his branch to rock it up and down.

From the ground rose an outraged cry, "Stop it! Are you mad?"

Percy Mullen called, "Gee, John. That's crazy. What d'you prove if you're dead?"

He slid through the branch with bleeding hands and dropped his feet to the bough. "I'll not do my model!" he yelled. "I'll not do my stupid old project."

He straddled the bough, then slid a leg over the side and rolled and held on by the armpits as before. The next branch was there, squarely in line, and he let go.

He jarred into splitting twigs and showering leaves, and scored a weal two inches long across his chin. He wallowed as though in water above his depth, he swayed, and shrieked, "Ahoy, there! Ahoy! I'm John Clement Sumner up a tree!" Then said with a devil in his eye, "Hi-ya, Constable Baird."

John leered through his leaves and wriggled to the bough. There were no nerves now, none at all, and he scrambled down to the policeman's feet.

There he looked up into a pale and agonized face and the policeman looked down on a flushed small boy (smaller than his years), bleeding, scratched, panting for breath, laughing in a peculiar way that no one but the policeman heard.

John unlaced the boot that was caught in the crease of the bough. It wasn't easy, because tying up laces and undoing them was like writing words with a pen. He fumbled, he trembled and shook, but not with nerves of fear, not with stammering, not with shame, and went over the edge to the next bough down before the policeman realized his foot could move.

"John," he called quietly, with a forced and unnatural calm.

"Yes, sir."

"Wait, boy, please. We must tie ourselves together. You're not well enough to go down alone."

John went down, from branch to branch and bough to bough, weaker at the knees than a child of three, dripping with rain, soaked with sweat, smeared with blood, but singing in his heart and sometimes out loud. It was like something out of a dream, but so real, so real. He was there but a thousand miles away.

He heard a scream, but it wasn't his own.

He knew that he had fallen but knew nothing more.

12

Stranger in the House

Was it a morning like other mornings? There were bird sounds but no traffic sounds; there was light but not sunlight; and not a whisper of breeze moving in the curtains. Everything was still; everything seemed to be dead except for the birds and for the slow, deep breathing of a creature he could not see.

Percy Mullen's dogs were not barking; Sissy Parslow's axe was not chopping; no sound of Mum or Dad came from the kitchen. He could hear the clock, but couldn't see it; he peered towards it, squinting, but its face was indistinct.

Something was wrong. There was a half-remembered dream of a tree, of exhausting emotion, of voices shouting and calling, of a ladder, of falling through darkness past stars and planets and moons. He hated dreams of falling. Sometimes he fell for hours. Sometimes he woke up screaming, but he wasn't screaming now. He woke up sitting, hot and creepy with perspiration.

He felt sore and sick. Was he ill again, waking from a fever? His dream had been violent and he still stung from its scratches.

"Oh, John Clement Sumner," Mum would say, "your imagination will be the death of me. Just look at you. Can't you spend a night in bed without fighting lions with your claws?"

There was a chair beside the bed and Mum was in it, in her dressing-gown, head drooping forward as though her neck was made of rubber. He stared at her for an indefinite time, hazy in his mind, realizing that it was her breathing he had heard. He couldn't change her into a bear, or a burglar, or an invisible man. Mum was always Mum; always there.

She woke suddenly as though prodded with a pin, and perhaps looked giddy (though it was hard to say), and touched her forehead with an unsteady hand. "Oh dear," she said, "is it morning?" Then sighed heavily and rubbed her eyes. "Hullo, darling. Awake, I see."

After that she said nothing for a time except for odd little sighs. She looked lost. In a while she ran her fingers through her hair, nervily tidying it, then straightened her gown and opened the curtains wide as she did for any other day.

It was very early indeed; by the clock only 5:23.

"You've slept for seventeen hours," she said, and stood silhouetted against the early day. Something about her was odd, almost unreal. Somehow her eyes caught the light, perhaps from the mirror. She looked strange.

"Are you hungry?" she asked, but he didn't hear.

He was feeling himself all over, frowning, restless, creaking the bed.

"Mum. . . . It wasn't a dream."

"No, John. It was not."

"Seventeen *hours!*"

"Exhaustion, they call it. Twelve-thirty yesterday the doctor carried you into bed. I was home soon after one, your father with me. One way and another it was quite a day."

"I *really* climbed the tree?"

There was an exaltation in him. He could have

grown wings and leapt into the sky.

"Yes, John."

"And really got down?"

"I suppose you'd call it that. Yes, you got down."

Dad came into the room, in pyjamas, looking tired. "Hullo, stranger," he said. "You certainly gave us a scare. It was a pretty good effort, John Sumner, for a boy who can't climb."

Then everything went quiet again. If they were going to bellow at him he wished they'd start. He looked at them warily, his defences bristling. You could never trust grown-ups when they were quiet, when they purred like cats. Then he put his feet to the floor.

"No, no. You stay there. You spend today in bed." But Mum corrected herself. "Get out if you want to. Do as you please."

That stopped him, rather than encouraged him. It bewildered him in a way, and for no reason that he knew of he thought suddenly, guiltily, of a loaf of bread sitting on a chair. "I left the bread in the rain!"

Dad seemed to blink, but Mum said, "Bread, he says; he left it in the rain. And his pants on the line, too. Is that all you've got to say for yourself?"

Dad touched Mum's arm. "Easy, dear," and everything went quiet again.

John felt awfully embarrassed; just as in his dreams of walking down Main Street without any clothes on. "I'm hungry," he said, and swallowed hard. He wasn't very steady and leant against the bed. "Golly, seventeen hours."

They smiled at him, but he distrusted them profoundly.

"Can I have cold milk on my Wheaties?"

"You know that hot milk is the rule."

Yeh; that was more like it, wasn't it? The *rule.*

"Did I bounce when I fell?"

It was funny the way that question came out. He hadn't thought of it at all; it was suddenly there.

"They said you fell as if the tree wasn't there. That you were holding on even as you fell to something that wasn't there. They thought you were dead; that you were dead even then; lying on the pillows. It's a wonder . . ."

Dad stopped her again, with his hand, then said, "I think breakfast is a jolly good idea. It's not too soon to start the day."

But Mum couldn't hold herself back. "Why did you do it, John? Why? Aren't you going to tell us?"

Dad grabbed her arms, but it was too late.

"I'll not be silenced. I'll not be told what I'm to say. The years I've given to this child! The things you shouted up in that tree. The things I've had to take from people."

"*Stop it!*" Dad had her by the shoulders, fiercely, but not angrily. "*Stop it, dear.*"

"Those *people.*"

John didn't know what to do, except scramble back into bed.

"They're not *all* like that," Dad said. "Be fair."

"All the years I've given to John; all the years I've tried. All lost in a single day."

John tried to shut his ears; he hated it when Mum and Dad were like this. When Mum started crying it was awful. He couldn't think when Mum cried.

But Mum wasn't crying. She was making queer little movements with her hands. "I'm afraid yesterday has not been easy for me to understand; your father looks at it differently. For the life of me I don't know who's right; but I suppose I'll have to be wrong. If there's been a mistake somewhere, I suppose it's mine. Cold milk, you said, didn't you? With banana or cream?"

Suddenly her voice broke and suddenly she was not in the room.

Only Dad was left. Poor old Dad; he looked as though someone had hit him with a club; heavy shadows under his eyes and a hoarseness in his voice. "Oh, John," he said, "will you ever know what you have done?"

Dad sat on the bed, clasping his hands together. (Dad was a big man in his job; he didn't look it now.) He cleared his throat several times; with everything he said he cleared it more. "Parents have their problems, son; but they can forget that boys have problems, too. . . .

"The operation on your leg is off—at least for now. Mr. Macleod says we must see what happens; that it would be a crime to touch you. . . . No, you're not to say anything. You're to hear me out.

"Ordinary boys and girls get knocks and bruises you've never dreamt of. Ordinary people have to live with ordinary treatment, and that's not what you're used to. You've been given special treatment; I doubt if you'll ever know how *special* it has been. But I gather you've had your fill of it. You'd prefer the knocks and bruises."

John didn't know what to say to that, but Dad didn't seem to be putting a question. He was peering intently at his clasped hands.

"Let's see you stand on your own feet. Let's see if this works the trick. . . ." Dad was shaking his head. "Mr. Macleod suspects—he suspects. . . . Well, let's pray God that he's right. What are you going to do with this freedom? Abuse it, as you abused it yesterday, or are you going to see it as the chance to say *no* to yourself instead of hearing it from others? Do you want to get out into this rough and tumble? Come on, come on; I'm asking you."

John covered his eyes, not believing, scarcely understanding. "More than anything else in the world."

"All right; you may."

In a moment, Dad's fingers ruffled John's hair. "When you're ready, come through for breakfast."

Then Dad wasn't there and John's mind was empty; everything emptied out and ran away.

When he started thinking again there was an image in his thoughts of Sissy Parslow. No; not Sissy; *Cecil* was his name.